THE PLIGHT OF
NIMARA

THE PLIGHT OF NIMARA

TANYA BOURTON

AuthorHouse™ UK Ltd.
1663 Liberty Drive
Bloomington, IN 47403 USA
www.authorhouse.co.uk
Phone: 0800.197.4150

© 2014 Tanya Bourton. All rights reserved.

No part of this book may be reproduced, stored in a retrieval system, or transmitted by any means without the written permission of the author.

Published by AuthorHouse 08/11/2014

ISBN: 978-1-4969-8915-4 (sc)
ISBN: 978-1-4969-8914-7 (hc)
ISBN: 978-1-4969-8916-1 (e)

Any people depicted in stock imagery provided by Thinkstock are models, and such images are being used for illustrative purposes only.
Certain stock imagery © Thinkstock.

This book is printed on acid-free paper.

Because of the dynamic nature of the Internet, any web addresses or links contained in this book may have changed since publication and may no longer be valid. The views expressed in this work are solely those of the author and do not necessarily reflect the views of the publisher, and the publisher hereby disclaims any responsibility for them.

In memory of my sweet Granny.
You are forever in my heart.

Contents

Chapter 1	The Bus	1
Chapter 2	Trapped	4
Chapter 3	Granddad	7
Chapter 4	Underground Life	11
Chapter 5	The Attack	14
Chapter 6	The Nightmare	16
Chapter 7	The Great Hall	18
Chapter 8	Experience is Everything	21
Chapter 9	Reunited	24
Chapter 10	Prepare to Fight	28
Chapter 11	No Pain, No Gain	32
Chapter 12	Solidarity	36
Chapter 13	The Lessons Begin	39
Chapter 14	Standing on the Shoulders of Giants	44
Chapter 15	Brutal Truths	46
Chapter 16	Training Begins	49
Chapter 17	Pushed Too Far	52
Chapter 18	A Little Faith	55
Chapter 19	The Pill	60
Chapter 20	Time to Think	63
Chapter 21	Farewell, My Friends	66
Chapter 22	The Voyage into Space	70
Chapter 23	Inside the Spaceship	73
Chapter 24	The Battle Plans	77
Chapter 25	The Test	80
Chapter 26	This is Nimara	83

Chapter 27	Into Battle	88
Chapter 28	Facing the Gwarks	92
Chapter 29	The Battle Continues	95
Chapter 30	Back in the City	98
Chapter 31	Remembrance	101
Chapter 32	Home	105
Chapter 33	The Bus	108

CHAPTER 1

THE BUS

UNFORTUNATELY, IT WAS an ordinary Monday morning. Bruno rushed out of the house, jumped over the gate as fast as a bolt of lightning, and skipped onto the waiting yellow bus. Panting, he sank into the black leather seat. The torn panel by his side spewed yellow foam like a dry tongue. Above the tongue, two crossed eyes had been drawn. Bruno smiled; he had drawn those eyes to impress the new girl that started at his school.

Sitting in his favourite seat, he thought back to that day, and a smile played on his lips. He remembered every detail with such clarity and ran them through his mind. That day the sun had shone a brilliant white, and the first buds of spring were opening on the trees lining the road. The breeze had gently caressed everything in its path.

The bus pulled to a stop; the engine vibrated, ready to continue its voyage. And there she was: a radiant angel, a goddess from an unknown world, a graceful nymph that seemed so out of place on the grubby bus. The sun's beams that followed her made glitter of her flowing blonde hair. Her eyes were ocean-blue pools of mysteries yet to be told. Her movements were a contrast of strength and vulnerability.

When she turned to find a seat, her eyes settled on Bruno and she smiled. That smile caused time to stop, and all noise ceased at once. Bruno's heart drummed uncontrollably within the confines of his rib cage that served as its prison. She gravitated towards him.

Bruno was paralysed in his seat, unable to say a word. Her beauty had numbed him to the core. She sat in the vacant seat opposite his. Only the pathway kept them apart.

It took him a good ten minutes to compose himself and find the courage to engage in some conversation with her. Her name was Summer, which Bruno felt was so apt.

He searched for his pen, which was at the bottom of his bag, and finding it, he drew the eyes on his seat and sheepishly gave her a cheeky grin. Her laughter was music to his ears and filled him with pride to see that she found his antics amusing. The sun shone as brightly inside his heart as it did outside.

The bus jogged along, hopping over the lumps and bumps in the road, causing Bruno to snap back to reality. Rubbing his eyes, he stared at his ghostly reflection in the dirty window. His ginger hair was tussled, and a tiny sprinkle of freckles looked carelessly tossed across his small, straight nose. His eyes were his best feature; everyone told him so. His were kind eyes that vividly expressed emotions. Was it not Summer who told him it was easy to see what he was thinking? 'All I have to do is stare into your eyes'. He could almost hear those words now and feel her touch as she gently placed her hand under his chin. His lips were puckered in thought. He wondered where Summer was now. Just when they had started to get to know each other, she'd disappeared. It was as if she had never gone to his school at all.

The bus jolted once more. This time Bruno's stomach lurched. The bus seemed to be going faster than usual, and the engine roared angrily, choking on its exhaust fumes.

Bruno noticed other differences from the usual journey. It smelled clinical, like a dentist's reception. It felt cold inside, even though there was no air conditioning. It was very silent, odd for a bus full of fourteen-year-old kids on a Monday morning. Bruno felt a shiver crawl up his spine. A tight cramp gripped his throat, and he found it hard to swallow. Something was definitely wrong.

He turned around and saw the other passengers around him and now faced the boy behind. Bruno's eyes widened; his face became a marble statue, and his lips trembled. As he stared at the boy, the boy stared straight back.

'We look the same', Bruno whispered, and then gave a nervous laugh that sounded close to a whimper.

The boy replied in monotone, 'Yes, we look the same', and smiled back eerily.

As if this was a trigger, right on beat, everyone on the bus voiced in unison, 'Yes, we all look the same', and stared at Bruno.

Chapter 2

TRAPPED

As through a sea of green mist – weightless, devoid of thought or emotion – Bruno let himself be carried along by the hypnotic waves between dream and consciousness. The will to wake was a distant memory as exhaustion and fear held him captive. To remain oblivious to the horrors that awaited him felt like a protective cocoon that shielded him and forbade him to accept his fate. Ignorance was bliss.

His heart beat to the rhythm of a silent melody. Its gentle thumping aided his sleep. However, something deep within called to him, urged him to open the Pandora's Box of his mind. Bruno was aware that once it was opened, the memories – memories that he would rather stayed hidden, forgotten, buried in the seabed – of what occurred on the bus would be released, cascading in a tidal wave. The clinical smell became more apparent, and Bruno was transported once more onto the bus.

The eerie smile on the boy's face turned into a wide grin, showing sharp, pointed teeth. The face, which was like his own, appeared to melt and mould into something inhuman. Bruno felt weak and trembled uncontrollably. His face drained of blood, and then the dark provided a blanket.

Bruno fainted.

*

The swirl of memories intertwined, becoming more confused. A white light shined into his eyes, steel handcuffs secured him in a leather chair, warm soapy water gushed down like a strong shower, and hard brushes painfully rubbed his body.

'What happened to me?' The question escaped in a thin whisper. It hung in the air unanswered.

Once more Bruno surfaced from his cocoon. This time he felt a little stronger, a little more curious about his surroundings, and much more determined to discover the answer to his question.

He repeated in a low, controlled voice that was heavy with conviction, 'What happened to me?' Lifting his eyelids, he attempted to work out where he was. His vision was blurred, and he could only make out odd shapes, none of which moved. His other senses were clear. He still smelled the clinical odour, although now it was more pronounced. He sat with his back against a wall. Surprisingly the wall was not hard and cold but soft and radiating warmth. The floor was soft too and reminded him of the thick-pile carpet at home. Home ... never before had the word filled him with such sorrow. It caused a dull ache in his stomach and a tightening in his throat. Tears pricked his eyes as he pictured his parents smiling at him.

Swiping a hand across his eyes cleared his vision. Blurry shapes took solid form. A table with a jug of water and two tall glasses had been placed in the centre of the room. Alongside the table were two steel chairs. The water tempted Bruno, its obvious temperature visible in the rivers that ran down the side of the monumental jug and the crystal-clear cubes of ice that settled motionlessly, suspended like icebergs. Bruno licked his dry, cracked lips, failing to moisten them. He eyed the water greedily.

The room itself was of a comfortable size; large enough to breathe easily and small enough to feel cosy. Everything was a bland shade of cream and void of decoration, and it was immaculately clean.

'What kind of prison is this?' Bruno murmured. His hands and feet were not chained and he felt no pain. His eyes were drawn back to the water. Small droplets burst in friendly winks. Like a cautious hawk assessing its prey, Bruno considered whether or not to drink the water. Was it poisoned or was it safe?

His animal instinct took over and he swiftly swooped towards the table and pounced. Clutching the jug tightly between his claws, he buried his face in the rim and guzzled furiously. He lapped greedily as though to quench an inferno that burned aggressively inside. Water spilled over his cheeks and trickled down his throat, collecting in pools between his shoulder blades before falling freely to the floor. Only when the last sliver of water vanished did Bruno allow himself to gasp for air. Kneeling with his head bowed, the jar released to tumble away from him, he breathed. All thoughts were centred on the rise and fall of his chest and the wonderful sensation of steady revitalisation. A new awakening brought fresh energy; all senses became acute, and thinking was made possible. Running his hand through his hair, Bruno raised his face to the ceiling, and with closed eyes, he sighed with satisfaction. Bruno felt more like himself; he felt ready to face the unknown.

'You do realise the glasses were put there for a purpose, boy?'

Bruno's eyes became circles. His breath halted in its tracks, caught in the back of his throat, refusing to be expelled into the air. He slowly turned towards the sound of the voice. In the corner, almost camouflaged by the cream-coloured garments that matched the rest of the room, was an old man. The first thing Bruno noticed was that the man had the kind of smile that extended to his eyes. Those eyes, although full of wisdom, overflowed with the sort of energy associated with youth. And was his smile just a little tainted with sarcasm?

Chapter 3

GRANDDAD

THE OLD MAN folded his arms as if to relax further. Resting his head against the wall, he eyed Bruno carefully. 'I wondered when you were going to come to your senses. You have slept for three days'.

Bruno's cheeks flushed with embarrassment at the thought of how he must have appeared as he feverishly gulped the water. He had acted like an animal left out in the wild: untamed, feral, and unfit to be called human.

As if able to read his thoughts, the old man gave a soft laugh. 'Don't worry about the water; they'll bring more'.

'Who are "they"?' Bruno asked. Perhaps this man would be able to piece together the wild and perplexing ideas that were colliding in his mind. Perhaps he could make some sense of it all and erase some of the fear that shadowed his heart. How often had he heard that we fear the unknown? Bruno now understood that phrase more than ever before, but was he really ready for the unknown to become known? Ignorance was still bliss, and that phrase felt more comforting and safe.

The old man sighed and slowly stood. As he stretched, pain was etched across his face, and he grimaced. He plodded towards the table.

Bruno watched every movement with wonder as though looking at a sage idolised for his wealth of knowledge. The old man steadily sat in one of the chairs. Once settled, he gestured for Bruno to do the same.

'I will tell you as much as I know, which is not as much as I would like. Believe this – you will have to trust in what I say and in order to do this you must forget what you have ever learnt about truth, reality, myth, or laws of possibility. Once I start to talk just listen. When I have finished, you will not be the same boy that faces me now'.

Bruno was spellbound by the calm, gentle tone of the old man's voice. 'Start talking, Granddad; I'm listening'. With this Bruno settled in the chair opposite.

The old man started. 'There is not an easy way to say this. We have been taken by aliens and are locked up in a facility underground. Just above us, I believe, are the Moors in Devon. The Aliens want to be as discreet as possible and so chose such a desolate place. We are still on Earth Bruno, just in case you thought we were on some distant planet. From what I can gather, there are other people locked up here too. I can hear footsteps and talking; once I heard someone crying. The aliens have not harmed me in any way, and it appears they have not hurt you. I believe they are not violent and have other uses for us. I can only speculate what these uses might be, but I doubt it has anything to do with conducting experiments or dissecting us to see how we tick. I think they want to learn from us, perhaps study our behaviour. I don't know why we were chosen. Maybe there are different reasons for each person here. All I know for sure is that there is no escape. The room is locked using a sophisticated device that I have never seen before'.

Bruno stared disbelievingly at the man. 'Aliens?' Just saying the word was completely ridiculous.

'Aliens', the man answered as if to confirm Bruno had heard correctly.

Bruno thought back to the day on the bus. It seemed like a lifetime ago, but just thinking about it made him shiver. The haunted nightmares were fresh in his mind. The image of the melting face, those sharp teeth caused Bruno to shut his eyes in an attempt to rid of them forever. 'How do you know there are other people like us locked up here? Those footsteps and crying could be the aliens'.

Without hesitation the man replied. 'They told me I was the oldest person taken'. At this he gave a shy grin that, for a brief moment, Bruno could almost see the young man he once was.

'I guess that means I won't find a girlfriend while I'm here'. His attempt at humour was not met with any warmth. 'Don't look at me like that', he continued defensively. 'I may be old but I do have feelings. Everyone wants to be loved, and everyone needs to be wanted'. With this, the man lowered his head to focus on his feet as if he had revealed too much of his own thoughts.

To Bruno it made him seem a desolate man.

'When the aliens took me I was a breath away from death. My wife had died, and I had nowhere else to go. We looked after each other, you see; we had a reason for living. We had each other. I was alone after she went away'. His voice broke at the memory of what had been lost. The pain had never gone away but remained, pushed aside by the need to get through day by pointless day. Just thinking about his wife – her voice, her smile, her embrace, anything and everything about her – caused the pain to resurface and twist like a knife in his heart.

His eyes became moist, and he sucked in breath in order to be more in control of himself. If he did not do so then he would regress into a piteous mess on the floor and would bawl inconsolably. 'Our children felt I would be an annoyance and too much trouble. I watched them argue over who should be responsible for looking after me, who had the bigger house, who had more time, and who was more patient and had learnt compassion skills. I ask you, patience? I'm their father, not a stranger, and as for compassion skills … how can you learn compassion? Watching them fight about this made up my mind. I moved to an old people's home. I gave the children the house and any savings I had left. I didn't need any of it. I'd made up my mind to die, and you don't need money where I hoped to go'. All this came out in a rush of emotion.

He continued. 'The only thing that really hurt was that they all told me I had chosen to do the right thing. No one tried to stop me. They were happy for me to die'. This final sentence was said calmly but was punctured with bitterness and such sorrow that Bruno felt uncomfortable. He shifted his gaze towards the pitcher which was now empty.

'The night the aliens came, I had completely given in and was ready to be reunited with Sophie, my wife. I felt oddly calm and listened to the clock ticking away my last moments on earth. A bright light slithered through the crack under the door and slowly filled the room until I had to shield my eyes from the brightness. I thought this must be it. I was ready to die.

'Then two shadows came towards my bed. They looked tall and thin, but that was all I could make out. They whispered to each other, and one gently took my hand and held it almost lovingly. I suddenly felt so weary, and sleep called out to me. I remember asking the angels to lead me to Sophie, and then I drifted off with the feeling of being lifted into the air and carried in cradling arms.

'When I woke up I was sad to see I wasn't with Sophie but in this room. It was later that I learnt that these angels were in fact aliens. Believe me, it was a huge disappointment. At first I thought they had chosen me because they wanted to know about death. Then I realised this could not be the case as they had, in fact, given me life. They talked to me and asked questions about my life. They were genuinely interested. Well, ever since my wife left me for a better place, no one took any notice of me. It was as though I was invisible. All of a sudden I was noticed. Okay, they aren't human but who cares? They need me in some way. That's all that matters. They need me'.

'You speak to them?' Bruno asked. With each new explanation, the nightmare he was in seemed to be growing increasingly insane.

'They want to talk to you too'. The man brightened. 'Oh, and you know you called me Granddad before?'

Bruno quickly tried to apologise, but with a simple gesture of his hand, the old man signalled for him to stop. 'Please call me that. I like it. I've always wanted to be called Granddad'.

Frowning, Bruno asked, 'Don't you have any grandkids?'

The old man smiled pitifully. 'Yes, but they never called me Granddad. In fact, they never called me anything at all'.

CHAPTER 4

UNDERGROUND LIFE

THE ROOM FELL into a thoughtful silence that, considering the previous conversation, felt oddly comfortable.

'By the way, my name is Bruno'.

After a pause, Granddad replied, 'Nice to meet you, Bruno'. He smiled warmly and patted Bruno on the shoulder.

Suddenly there was a hissing noise similar to that of a pressure cooker releasing steam. Both of them looked towards the sound coming from the door.

'It's them', Granddad said almost excitedly.

Icy fingers swept across Bruno's body, and he pinched his lips until they were thin, white lines. He was scared.

The door swished open, gliding on invisible hinges. Through the door, three figures emerged. Each one was the same height and similar in physique; they were small, almost fragile in quality. In any other situation Bruno would have laughed at the fact that these creatures, which he feared so much, were comic versions of aliens.

Their heads, obviously too large for the frame that supported them, were clumsily held aloft on thin wiry necks, and they bobbed with the weight. Their eyes were large orbs of crystal that hypnotically reflected the spectrum of light. Their slight mouths were slits under two holes that served as nostrils. Although they were humorous in looks, Bruno found them strangely beautiful.

One of them stepped forward and, like the door, seemed to glide effortlessly, closing the distance between them. He blinked and Bruno noticed that the skin of his eyelids were delicate lace and barely concealed the eyes beneath. He could distinctly smell the same clinical aroma that he had done on the bus and vaguely in the room. Obviously these were the beings that took him on that cursed day, but they had looked nothing like this.

Almost in a blur, the alien's face took on the likeness of Bruno, and the rest of the body followed suit. Suddenly Bruno was looking at what appeared to be his reflection. The reflection smiled and then returned to its original form.

'They will not show you their true form, Bruno', Granddad explained. 'They told me it was too stressful for you. You fainted'.

Bruno could hear the tone was deliberately mocking and felt the heat rush to his face, burning his ears and cheeks. 'Will they talk to me?' he asked quietly.

'We are looking forward to speaking with you'. The alien in front of him had a brittle, reedy voice that quivered. His tone was flat and lacked emotion; however, there was gentleness to it. 'First we would like to show you around, both of you'.

Bruno asked, 'Why us?' And then, raising his voice, asked, 'Why were we chosen?'

The alien turned back towards him and calmly replied, 'You were not chosen. We chose at random'. With this, the alien exited the room, followed by the other two aliens. They left the door wide open. Bruno looked at Granddad and shrugged. The two of them joined the aliens in the corridor.

After walking through several tunnel-like corridors, all of which were painted in the same cream colour, they came to a huge, frosted-glass archway which towered magnificently above them. The leading alien raised his long, thin hand, and the whole sheet of frosted glass rose up steadily, revealing a huge room beyond. The sheer brightness of the room caused Bruno and Granddad to raise their hands to their foreheads to shield their eyes. Gradually, getting used to the sudden brightness, they lowered their hands and stared in awe. Never in all their wildest dreams could they have created such a picture as what faced them now. Like stone statues they stared, soaking in every single detail, sucking in the atmosphere, and feasting on the brilliance of it all.

The gigantic hall was pure white with two sets of stairs sweeping up to a balcony high above. The stairs were encrusted with diamonds that shined like stars, throwing beams of light across the floor. On closer inspection, intricate patterns of gold snaked the banisters, which were seated firmly on vast gold pillars. The floor itself was solid marble, polished and adorned with an array of precious stones. Although luxurious, the patterns remained delicate, sophisticated, as though created by God himself. Huge red-velvet curtains flowed freely above the balcony, and even the curtain rods were carved into detailed shapes of various animals, all of which stared curiously at the people below. The hustle and bustle of the room itself was magical.

The room was filled to the brim with aliens and humans working diligently on a variety of tasks. There was much murmuring of enthusiastic chatter and lively debates.

Boom! A rocket shot towards the ceiling and exploded into a multicoloured shower that fell silently, bowing to its audience. The room erupted into great applause. Elsewhere, a loud crack was followed by a burst of black smoke that filled the air and slowly pirouetted until it vanished.

Tucked away in the corner of the room, an alien and a human concentrated on potions that bubbled frantically in glass vials. These rested precariously over bellowing Bunsen burners which were emitting a mirage of intense blue fire. The contents of each glass rapidly changed colour: from green to orange to yellow and finally to bright red. The alien picked up one of the vials and tipped the glowing contents over the table. Like parasites it consumed the solid metal beneath until the table broke and fell to the floor in pieces. This amused the alien, and he made a merry little dance in celebration.

A mosaic of action rattled across the whole room, and Bruno and Granddad attempted to see it all.

'Now it's time to talk'. The alien gave a melancholic smile and started back towards the room that was to be Bruno and Granddad's home for the unforeseeable future.

CHAPTER 5

THE ATTACK

THE ALIEN SAID, 'Imagine a world far beyond this galaxy, surrounded by three moons and two suns. The season is constant, neither hot nor cold but continuously comfortable. The flowers grow in abundance, and all animals roam free. There is only one nation as all people are admired for their differences. It is these differences that make them all beautiful. There is no need for hierarchy as each person knows his or her strengths and is respected for personal talents.

"This is the planet we are from; it is called Nimara. We are a peaceful nation that has not had negative emotions for centuries. There have been no disputes, murders, or wars for a long time'. The alien became woefull and dropped his head.

'This sounds like Utopia to me. So why are you so sad?' Granddad asked, interested to hear more.

'We are under attack'. The alien paused as if to show the severity of the situation. 'There is a nearby planet whose people are the complete opposite of ours – the Gwarks, as they are called. We have strived to make our world one of peace; they have fought to nurture one of chaos and disorder. Unfortunately, they have succeeded in this and now want to destroy our existence. We seem to enrage them, as they feel utter contempt for who we are'.

'How are we involved in all this?' Bruno asked.

'We have studied your planet for a long time and have always been curious about your ability to abuse and destroy. The various strategies you have devised over time to hurt and murder are a constant shock to us. The word "genocide" did not exist here, and the mere thought of such a thing to be possible can only be called pure evil. Such hatred between brothers and sisters is beyond our comprehension. Only your kind can help us beat the Gwarks, as your level of repulsion and savagery cannot be touched by any other world. We have lost the ability to fend for ourselves, so we must learn from the worst: you'.

'Thanks for the compliment', Granddad uttered, although in his heart he knew there was some truth in what the alien was saying.

Ignoring the comment, the alien continued, 'What you saw in the great hall is a wonderful example of how your kind is already helping us. With your pleasure of things destructive and our scientific intelligence, the ultimate weapons are being created'.

'We already have created the ultimate weapon: nuclear bombs', Bruno retorted.

The alien looked at Bruno and brushed aside the pathetic attempt at superiority. 'We want to stop the Gwarks, not eliminate them from existence'.

The alien turned to the two patient observers who until now had remained in a dignified silence. All three began to communicate in a flood of guttural sounds. At times they stopped to look at the two waiting humans as though pondering important ideas.

Finally the alien returned. 'Tonight you rest, and tomorrow morning you will be escorted to the great hall to share your knowledge with us'.

As if to prevent any further discussion, all three swished out of the room. With a hiss, the door slid shut.

Bruno and Granddad were left to stare dumbfounded at the door.

CHAPTER 6

THE NIGHTMARE

THAT NIGHT, BRUNO fell into a deep sleep filled with strange dreams. He was walking across a field. It was nighttime, and a strong but warm wind blew, lifting his hair and drying out his eyes. The ground was dusty; its surface danced as the wind threw it around. The trees stood like soldiers as their branches clawed the air. The cloudless sky allowed the stars to observe the world below. Two suns and three moons shined proudly, providing much-needed light as the scene was void of electric lighting.

Suddenly from behind, a loud scream and a stampede of feet hitting the ground erupted. Bruno whipped 'round to see a herd of aliens charging towards him. Their misshapen faces further contorted with rage. The noise was not unlike thunder as they hurtled, closing the distance. They were armed with guns that shot lightning beams. As these beams hit any solid surface it sizzled and ate away at the object until it vanished. Bruno realised he too held such a gun in his hand and it felt familiar to the touch.

Looking into the distance, he could see the enemy. They were charging fiercely in his direction. Tall and heavily built masses of muscle, they ran with athletic dexterity. Each carried a different weapon, all of which looked extremely dangerous and able to kill with ease. Their faces were hog-like and were fixed with determination and such hatred that Bruno felt himself quiver with fear. They were hell bent on extermination.

His side had caught up with him, and he was pulled along with the tide of aliens. Feet barely touching the ground, he howled a battle cry and held up his gun.

Both sides collided with such force that those in the front were instantly crushed to death. Blood gushed like geysers, drenching the next row of warriors. Weapons rained down, striking, slashing, and slaying anyone in its path.

Bruno fired the gun consistently and watched with pleasure as the enemy bellowed with pain, clutching wounds as hot blood frothed and then bubbled. With agonisingly slow speed, each victim melted to nothing. Only the red stains of death served as a memory of their existence.

Bruno raised his face to the sky and once more howled excitedly. As he did, his face turned into a wide grin, showing sharp, pointed teeth. The face appeared to melt and mould into something inhuman. He was one of the aliens.

Covered in sweat and hollering loudly, Bruno sat upright in his bed and panted, heart thumping wildly in his chest. It was dawn.

Chapter 7

THE GREAT HALL

Bruno and Granddad were ready an hour before the aliens entered their room. They sat side by side staring at the bare wall. Neither spoke a word, but they knew their thoughts were similar. Both were curious about the day ahead and what it would bring. Both were anxious and fidgeted subconsciously, unaware of the annoying repetitive movements of the other. Bruno twiddled his fingers whilst Granddad tapped his feet.

As the aliens came in, both stood up and waited for instruction.

'Follow us', was the greeting.

Soon they were back at the great hall, and even though it was their second visit, its beauty did not fail to leave them in awe.

For the first time since waking up in this place, Bruno and Granddad were separated. Each was assigned a different task. Like a young child being taken through the school gates, Bruno glanced back at Granddad with uncertainty. He had begun to think of him as his shelter, shielding him from any harm. He relied and trusted him implicitly.

'Granddad'. He smiled. 'Don't work too hard'. Bruno gave a nervous grin and delighted in the fact that Granddad gazed back at him with sincere affection as he was gently led away by another alien.

Bruno was escorted away in the opposite direction and through a door leading to yet another room. He took in his surroundings. This room was smaller than the great hall but in no way less interesting.

Highly polished wooden panels surrounded the entire length of each wall. The light bounced off the walls, giving them a mirror-like quality. Bruno realized this was an amphitheatre. White steps led to a stage below. The room itself was round so that all focus was on the stage. A group of aliens sat quietly on the bottom step, and even from this height Bruno felt an underlining sense of excitement and anticipation running through the group.

As he descended the steps, all eyes swept towards him. Bubbles of enthusiastic murmuring intensified into a crescendo of cheers. They had been waiting for this moment for some time. The feeling of nervousness burned like embers as Bruno advanced towards the stage. Uncertainty swept through him. His mind screamed, *What is this?* Finally he stood in front of the aliens, unsure of what was expected of him.

One of the aliens moved forward to greet him. 'Your task is to teach us how to fight. We have studied the human ability to enter combat without the use of weapons. Show us how this is done successfully'.

At this, all the aliens chorused, 'Teach us'.

Bruno stared at them, mouth open. After a brief pause, he replied, 'Teach you to fight? I'm not exactly brilliant at it myself'.

Frowning, the alien retorted, 'When you were eight you punched a boy in the playground and caused his nose to bleed. You also went to karate classes for a year. You can do more than we can'.

'How do you know about the fight when I was eight?' Bruno moaned.

The alien blinked, 'Research'. He shrugged and gave a broad grin.

Bruno stepped onto the stage. This caused a loud burst of applause, and the aliens bobbed up and down in their seats, eager to learn new skills.

Without hesitation, the alien at the end of the row jumped up and levitated gracefully onto the stage. He placed himself opposite Bruno and smiled up at him, full of admiration. Bruno put up his fists, expecting the alien to copy. The alien lowered his gaze to Bruno's hands, which were clenched so tightly, the knuckles turned white.

The alien raised his own hands, looked at them, and then lowered them to his sides where they dangled uselessly. Once more he stared at Bruno in wide-eyed wonder.

Okay, here goes. Bruno punched the alien lightly on the forehead. Even though the contact was gentle, it stunned the alien. He flinched, his hands shot up to his forehead, and his lips turned downwards. He whimpered but kept his attention on Bruno. The look he gave was like a wounded animal, pitifully begging to be released. His whimper turned to heartbreaking sobs, and he flopped back to his seat.

'Next'.

There were a few moments of silence. The second alien made his way to the stage; all excitement had obviously disappeared. He approached Bruno with trepidation, the fear visible in his saucer-shaped eyes. Having learnt from the previous victim, he held his hands high in pathetic fists. Bruno stepped forward and kicked one of his ankles. This caused the alien to stumble, and in an attempt to regain his balance, he frantically flapped his arms. He landed heavily on his backside and shrieked with surprise. The alien returned to his seat, rubbing his sore bottom.

Bruno looked around the room. 'Anyone else?'

There was a quick rumbling of conversation amongst the rest of the aliens. It was clear they had had enough for one day.

'I think you need better opponents to fight against', the first alien said. 'It may be best if we watch and learn for a while'. The moment he said these words, the others seemed to visibly relax.

The door at the top of the stairs opened, and the noise from the great hall rushed in. Someone stepped through the door and started to descend the stairs. At first the figure was a shadow, and then an outline of a human. Upon closer inspection, it became clear it was female.

Bruno started to make out features that were familiar to him. The light made glitter of her flowing blonde hair. Her movements were a contrast of strength and vulnerability.

Slowly she gravitated towards him. Bruno was paralysed, unable to say a word. Her eyes settled on Bruno and she smiled. 'Bruno?' she whispered.

'Summer!'

CHAPTER 8

EXPERIENCE IS EVERYTHING

GRANDDAD SAT COMFORTABLY in a white leather chair that cuddled him like a huge duvet. He sipped whisky from a crystal glass loaded with ice cubes. The liquid felt cool to his lips and coated his throat with a mild heat that anesthetised any soreness. He stared at the alien. There was a peaceful silence that helped him relax. He felt his weak bones revelling in this sudden break. His aches and pains dwindled away, partly due to the effects of his drink but also due to the soft support of the chair. His thoughts kept returning to the last time he saw Bruno. The image of the boy's face so full of fear made him appear younger than his fourteen years. His eyes were wide and pleading, making him appear smaller, more vulnerable.

'Harry', he finally said, 'Bruno is being treated well, isn't he?'

The alien gave a look that expressed, 'What do you think?' He rolled his eyes and looked at Granddad once more.

'It's just … he's a young boy,' Granddad continued.

Harry, as Granddad nicknamed him, smiled. 'He is fine. In fact, he has found an old friend'. His smile deepened. 'Funny how coincidences occur, but I do like a romance'. His small laugh jolted his thin frame.

Granddad was suspicious that anything that happened here was never a coincidence. He placed the glass on the table, which was positioned at arm's reach. He noticed his hands had begun to shake again. Even aliens could not prevent nature's course. He was glad to have been allowed the extra time he was given and felt it would be wrong to expect more.

'Harry, we have met many times and have spoken at length about a variety of things, but …' Granddad paused to find the right words. 'I fail to see what help I am to you'.

Harry intensely observed his friend. 'I enjoy our conversations. I have learnt so much about your world and how humans think. Your vast knowledge is precious. In Nimara we live by the motto *Nanos gigantum humeris insidentes*: "One who discovers by building on previous discoveries"'.

'Ah!' Granddad said. '"If I have seen further, it is by standing on the shoulders of giants". Isaac Newton'.

'Do your young not stand on the shoulders of the old and wise?' Harry asked innocently.

Granddad's face grew long with sorrow as he thought about the dismissive behaviour of his children and grandchildren. They always had better things to do than speak to him. 'Unfortunately not. Some believe the old are foolish and have no worth at all on our planet. We are treated as though we have digressed to childhood'.

Harry listened fascinated by such idiocy. 'What a waste!' he exclaimed. 'Your planet will never progress. Your people will repeat mistakes again and again. It amazes me how long your planet has been around, yet the people who inhabit it are so …' He paused. 'Inferior'.

Granddad sat back and sighed, defeated. He knew there was no possible defence for mankind. The word 'inferior' bruised him. He voiced his thoughts. 'Well, we are all answerable to the man upstairs in the end. However, most do not seem to fear him either'.

Harry looked towards the ceiling, puzzled. Realization dawned over his face, and he erupted into a hearty laugh and involuntarily clutched his miniscule belly. 'You mean God'. He breathed slowly until his chuckles abated. 'Oh, even your language was created to deceive. You cannot say the truth but a distorted form of it'.

Feeling thoroughly inadequate under the assessment of this better being, Granddad quickly changed the subject and asked, 'How is the situation with the Gwarks?'

Harry looked off into the distance, deep in thought. Quietly he whispered, 'The Gwarks; the one nation that fills us with such dread. The situation appears futile. I do not hold much hope of survival if truth be known. They are so strong, so savage and they will not consider any attempt made to settle this peacefully. As I said before to you and Bruno, our only chance is to rely on the teachings of those more savage – your kind'. He lowered his head as if to relieve the weight of the world he held on his small shoulders. 'We are relying on the inferior; how ironic'.

This final thought was left to float in the air until it withered away.

'The Gwarks are preparing their voyage to Nimara; war is inevitable. Here, it seems that we are making slow progress. You should have seen what happened in the amphitheatre earlier. Bruno caused injury to two of my men; they were not only disappointed by their lack of progress but humiliated and shocked'.

Granddad gave a proud smirk at the mention of Bruno's name.

Harry was quick to pick up on this. 'You find this funny?'

'No, of course not', Granddad replied without hesitation. 'It's just so good to hear that Bruno is making himself useful. I've got to admit, I was worried how he would cope with all this'.

'You really have grown to like the boy and so quickly', Harry pointed out. 'Why?'

Granddad thought about this carefully. 'I don't know really. I guess at first it was because I felt protective towards him. He was so fragile, physically and mentally, when you first brought him in. Now he is the grandson I wish I had'.

With ease, Harry lifted himself out of his chair. It never ceased to amaze Granddad how elegant and agile these beings were, and how crude and clumsy he felt.

'You must rest now. Soon Bruno will be returning to your room. I imagine there will be lots to talk about'. With this, Harry gestured for Granddad to stand up. 'I will walk you back'.

Side by side they walked towards the door, which swished open to allow them to exit.

Chapter 9

REUNITED

'Bruno?' she whispered.

'Summer!' Bruno exclaimed.

All eyes were upon the pair as they stood face to face. They linked hands and explored each other, grabbing hold of the fact that their vision had not tricked them. They truly were together once more. Lost in that moment, they forgot that a row of aliens was watching intently, all eager to see what would happen next. The pair snapped back to reality by a polite cough from the leader. They turned their heads in his direction at the same time.

As though feeling like an intruder, interrupting something special, he grinned sheepishly and raised his shoulders in a kind of apology. 'I think maybe you two would like some time alone'.

'Please'. Bruno grinned and returned his attention to Summer. 'Where have you been? Where did you go?'

Summer placed her warm hand under his chin and smiled. 'All in good time'.

Feeling her gentle touch, her familiar, smooth tone of voice caused all of the tension that had welled up inside him to wash away. Bruno felt closer to home. She led him to an adjoining room opposite the door that led back to the great hall. Even though he found it difficult to tear his eyes away from Summer, he instantly felt a change in atmosphere. The previous room was cold, empty, and structured for business. This room was cosy. It was much smaller, and to his surprise, the floor was covered with a thick-pile carpet that felt like cashmere. The carpet was pastel blue, and glitter flickered brightly when picked up by the light of the flames in the fireplace. These flames were alive and swayed gently. When Summer looked at him, he saw the fire reflected in her eyes, giving them a sense of vitality. Its radiance made her even more beautiful.

A large sofa sat invitingly before the fireplace, and on a table a pitcher of coca-cola fizzed, bubbles popping energetically. Beside the pitcher was a plate of large, thick cookies, each one a different flavour. Bruno's stomach came to life. The smell that wafted in the air was tantalizing, cruelly teasing him to be distracted from the girl of his dreams. He had forgotten how hungry he was.

'We have so much to talk about'. Summer had regained his attention. She looked at the pitcher and took the two glasses next to it, filling them to the brim. Bruno eagerly accepted one of the glasses she passed to him. She took the plate and sat on the sofa. Placing the plate next to her, she lifted her feet off the floor and swung them to her side. Head resting on the plump cushion behind, she patted the seat beside the plate for Bruno to join her.

Like an excited puppy, he jumped onto the sofa, nearly knocking the plate off balance.

Laughing, Summer held on to the plate. Both chose a cookie and sat in silence eating and drinking and enjoying the very fact that they were in each other's company.

'Summer, what happened to you? You just suddenly disappeared. I tried to contact you, but it was as though no one remembered you. Even your brother, Alex, ignored my questions when I saw him at school. I thought I had done something wrong and you instructed him to not speak to me'.

Summer's expression became overcast by sadness. She looked at Bruno carefully, wondering how to explain. 'Bruno, I didn't know this at the time, but when the aliens abduct people, they erase them from the memory of those closest to them. By that I mean they make sure their family forgets their existence. They feel that it is kinder to do this than to leave them missing their loved ones or constantly wondering what became of them'.

'But we remember our families'.

'Yes, I know'. Her lips trembled. 'I don't like the fact that Mum and Dad no longer remember me. It's as though they never loved me at all'.

Bruno thought about his own family at home and understood immediately. In his mind, they would all be trying to find him, miss him, and would shower him with love when he returned. However, being erased made it so final. He reached out to Summer, and she let herself be folded in his arms. Together, in silence, they gave and accepted comfort as words could not begin to express the depths of their despair. They clung to each other, deep in thought. At that moment, the magic of just being with someone familiar was all they wanted and needed.

Summer began to speak and sounded far away as she revisited the past. 'Remember that afternoon when we said we would go to the cinema? I told you I would text you after my dance lesson'.

'Yes. How could I forget? You didn't text me'. His voice broke with all the emotions he had felt that evening. They surfaced in one explosion, pelting anger, panic, and sorrow. Anger as he felt she had cast him aside like an old, discarded toy; panic as she had let him down; and sorrow as he always believed he was not good enough for her. Now he held her even more tightly.

Summer reacted to the sudden tightness by doing the same. 'They took me while I was getting ready for my dance class. I was in the changing rooms fixing my hair into a ponytail. The other girls had already gone out into the corridor, waiting for our teacher to invite us into the main studio. I heard them laughing and talking about the forthcoming production'.

The memories of such happy times painted a smile on her face, making her entire countenance more relaxed. The pain and frustration of recent events were no longer etched in the creases of her brow or in the bleakness of her eyes.

'Mandy was the loudest', she said. 'She was so excited to be given the part of Titania. She always liked to play the beautiful characters, especially when they were in some way magical'. A short giggle escaped her lips and was quickly replaced with a more serious tone.

'I was facing the mirror at the time when another figure seemed to appear behind me. I saw it in the reflection. It did not appear suddenly, like it would if a person stepped up behind you, but materialised slowly. It began as a shadow that slowly took shape. I was frozen to the spot by fear and curiosity. I could see a face forming, a face that looked more like a hideous mask, with pointed teeth. Then it changed as it became more vivid. I blinked, thinking I was going insane. Was I having an aneurism? Was I going to die? I did not believe what I was seeing.

'When the shape became solid, I spun around but no one was there. I returned to the mirror and there it was, waiting for my attention. It smiled and held its hand out to me. The hand came out of the mirror. I don't know why, but it felt right to take the hand. As soon as I did I was pulled through the mirror. A blinding white light engulfed me. The next thing I remember was waking up in a room'.

Bruno listened intently, thinking how strange it was that everyone's experience was so different. 'You've been here for roughly five months', Bruno pointed out.

'Five months?' Summer couldn't believe it had been so long. 'No one mentions days or weeks here. Time seems to not really count'.

'Only the mission counts,' Bruno replied.

'Mission?' It was clear Summer was ignorant of what was going on.

Remaining in each other's arms, Bruno told her everything that he knew, starting with his first meeting with Granddad.

CHAPTER 10

PREPARE TO FIGHT

SUDDENLY AN ALARM began to whoop, gradually growing louder until it got to a painful volume and then stopped. Bruno looked at Summer and raised his eyebrow.

'It's time for dinner', she explained. 'You'll get used to it'.

Bruno replied, 'I never heard anything like that before'.

'No, you can only hear it from this part of the building. When you're in your room, the aliens believe you should be at peace and therefore should not be disturbed by any of the alarms'. She smiled and the whole room seemed to brighten.

To Bruno, nothing in the world could be more beautiful or heart-warming than that smile. He could honestly feel as though he could spend the rest of his life with her. If anyone had told him he would ever feel like this, he would have laughed; not anymore.

Summer interrupted his thoughts. 'Come on; let's go get something to eat'. Taking him by the hand once more, she gently led him through the door and along yet another corridor.

Bruno heard the hum of enthusiastic chatter and clinking of plates before he reached the room. The noise vibrated down the corridor and exploded into a welcoming melody as Summer excitedly pushed open the doors and skipped inside the room.

Bruno followed and could not believe the sight before him. Hundreds of people crowded around tables, laughing and talking whilst eating their meals. They all seemed to be at ease and enjoyed each others company. No matter what colour or race, they all got on very well together. All wore the same cream-coloured clothes, yet all were different. It was truly an amazing sight and one that he thought would never have been possible.

'Come on,' Summer urged, pulling him to join the queue. Like in a regular café, they each took a tray and waited their turn.

The aroma of various meals sent his stomach into overdrive and it rumbled ceaselessly. Bruno detected various meats and vegetables as well as an array of sauces. In the kitchen behind him, aliens were busy at work preparing dish after dish. They worked meticulously, and he watched with appreciation.

On the side table, various drinks lined up as though to attention, and light bounced off the glasses, spreading a rainbow of colours across the table. Bruno noticed how spotlessly clean the place was; the cutlery shined brilliantly, and the floor and tabletops had been meticulously washed and polished. Through the aroma of the many dishes that waited to be chosen, he made out the underlining smell of disinfectant. As he reached the front of the queue, the amount of choices was overwhelming. He took the plate closest to him and placed it on the tray. He did the same with his drink, and he and Summer found a place to sit.

Bruno closed his eyes and savoured the food with absolute pleasure. With a full mouth he cried, 'Oh this is just amazing!' He looked down at the plate and was sorry to see he had already managed to eat more than half the dish that had been generously piled a moment ago.

Giggling excitedly, Summer exclaimed, 'You think this is great? Just wait for pudding'.

'Bruno, Bruno … hey, hope you're okay,' Granddad shouted from across the room.

Bruno looked around, trying to find the source of the voice. As his eyes focused on Granddad, he leapt to his feet and waved eagerly. 'Hey, I'm fine. I have lots to tell you'.

Granddad gave him the thumb's up and went back to his conversation with the people sitting with him.

Summer introduced Bruno to the others at their table. Most were of a similar age to him but came from different countries. He was impressed by how well they all spoke English. At school, Bruno had tried to learn French but gave up very quickly as he found it too difficult. The other kids informed him that the aliens felt it would be more beneficial for everyone to keep to the English language because most humans had a good grasp of it.

The conversation soon turned to more serious matters as Carlos, an olive-skinned boy, said, 'I heard the Gwarks have already landed on Nimara'.

'I heard they had already started to fight', a petite and pretty blonde girl added reluctantly. Tears welled in her clear-blue eyes. Her name was Elzbieta.

Suddenly the room fell into silence and all attention turned to the alien that stood on the far end of the room. He held his hands up, gesturing for all to listen. Something about his demeanour shouted out bad news. 'I have been informed that the Gwarks have landed on Nimara'.

'See?' Carlos whispered sharply, to which the rest of the table hissed back for him to be quiet.

'They have taken control of the Great Tower building where our government live and work'. He paused and gave an almighty sigh. 'There were no survivors'.

The room erupted into chaotic chatter.

Once more the alien signalled for silence, and all responded at once.

'It is also believed the Gwarks have discovered our secret building here and have launched another ship. They are quite possibly heading for us as I speak'.

The room convulsed into susurration. Each person barked panicked remarks at each other. Fear was visible in everyone's eyes.

For the last time the signal for silence was given, but this time it took a few moments before complete attention returned to the alien.

'Tomorrow the alarm will sound in all rooms. You must all rise and be ready. You are no longer just helping us survive; you are now responsible for each other's survival. We are all in this together more so now than ever. Tonight, you must finish your meals and rest. Tomorrow we prepare to fight'.

With these last words, the alien bowed to wish everyone good night and left a silence that was filled with darkness.

After a brief moment, a small voice questioned apologetically, 'Pudding...anyone?' By the serving area, an alien stood with a spoon clenched high above his head. He smiled meekly, pleading for a more enthusiastic response than he was receiving.

Even though the mood was completely dampened by the dreadful news, Bruno had to admit the pudding was unbelievably more amazing than the main meal.

CHAPTER 11

NO PAIN, NO GAIN

GRANDDAD WAITED EAGERLY for Bruno to return to the room. There were so many things Granddad wished to share. For so long he had remained a lonely man, and thought he had grown accustomed to keeping his thoughts to himself. However, meeting Bruno had completely changed that. He excitedly paced the room, often stopping to glance towards the door. His impatience was somehow filled with energy and keen expectation.

The door whooshed open.

Granddad took a deep breath to appear more composed. He relaxed and asked almost disinterestedly, 'Bruno, I hope you had an eventful day'.

Bruno shot into the room with a serious yet anxious look on his face. He too had waited agitatedly, the events of the day bursting to be told to his companion. 'Did you hear what was said in the dining hall?' he began at a pace that would gather momentum. 'The Gwarks are heading towards us. We aren't ready yet. How are we going to protect ourselves?'

The old man stopped Bruno in mid-flow. 'I know, I know, but just hold on a moment'. His raised yet calm voice had an air of authority that caused Bruno to listen. 'All these questions will be answered in good time'.

'But …' Bruno was ready to accelerate again, but the old man quickly prevented him.

'Wisely and slowly, they stumble that run fast', he quoted, looking at the boy's confused expression. 'Never mind. We've got time to make plans if they are indeed heading for us'. With this, he moved towards the table and sat comfortably in one of the chairs.

He raised his eyebrows as an invitation, and Bruno obediently placed himself in the other seat. 'Now what I want to know is who the pretty little girl is that you were with. You two seem very close'.

Bruno dipped his head shyly and blushed. He mumbled, 'She's Summer'. As he said her name, his mouth perked into a lopsided smile. He lifted his eyes to meet Granddad's; Bruno's shined brightly, searching for approval.

'Summer', Granddad repeated. He mouthed the name slowly as though assessing its worth. He too had a glint in his eye, but the quality of it was far more mischievous. 'That's a time of year, not a name'.

'Summer by name, summer by nature', Bruno retaliated.

'Oh, I do believe you have a soft spot for the young lady', Granddad teased.

Bruno turned crimson. 'I love her'. His voice was barely audible.

'Sorry? My ears are not as good as they were. What did you say?' Granddad asked, faking innocence.

'I'm in love with her', he repeated loudly. He looked at the old man, astonished by what he had just announced so boldly.

'That's what I thought you said … but you do not love her', the wise man chided. 'You like her a lot, anyone can see that, but love …love grows'. Saying this, Granddad floated away into the past. A forlorn look softened his features. His thoughts were focused on things only visible to the mind's eye.

Returning to the present, he gave a wistful smile. 'Yes, love grows, my boy, and I hope you will experience it one day. Love is like ivy. It's organic, wild, fierce yet beautiful. When it engulfs you, it blinds you, possesses you, yet it sets you free. Love is the most consuming of all emotions, a flame to a moth, a light in the dark. It needs nurturing. The strongest of all feelings, yet the one that needs the most gentle touch'.

He saw disappointment etched in Bruno's face. The look was set in determination, shouting out that he knew his own mind and knew where his heart lay.

Granddad said, 'Summer seems like a lovely girl; I would like to make her acquaintance properly. If she is important to you, then naturally she is important to me too'.

Bruno grinned widely and seemed to relax. 'I really do want you to meet her. It's just that after the news, I thought it would be inappropriate to bring her to your table'.

'Back to the news again'. Granddad sighed once more, although in truth he knew the subject could not be avoided. 'Tell me, how do you plan to teach the aliens to fight? I am aware that this morning did not go so well. What is your next tactic?'

Bruno became quiet and stared at the floor. 'I haven't thought of a plan yet. So much has happened since this morning'.

'Well, you'd better think of one quickly. It's your responsibility', Granddad fired back sharply. 'We all have our duties here, and if we're to survive, they need to be taken very seriously'.

Bruno felt he could not argue with the old man's words and remained silent. The burden of such responsibility weighed heavy and terrified the young boy.

The door swept open once more, and they turned to see who had interrupted their conversation.

Slowly, a wide eyed alien poked his bulbous head from behind the door and blinked at them. He turned his attention to Bruno and smiled nervously. Although feeling intimidated by the way the two humans stared at him, he hovered in the doorway.

'Charlie, just come in, will you?' Granddad gently called out to the alien.

'Charlie?' Bruno asked.

'Yes, this is Charlie, the one who you …' Granddad gestured towards his own face and grimaced.

Bruno realised this was the poor creature he had punched and turned to apologise. He took a step forward, and the alien protectively grasped his forehead. Even though it seemed impossible, his eyes grew wider with fear.

'I want to learn how to punch like that', the alien squeaked.

An idea started to brew, and Bruno allowed it to form into a coherent and solid thought. 'Charlie, tomorrow, first thing, you must meet me in the amphitheatre with five others of your choosing. Could you also inform Summer, Carlos, and Elzbieta to be there as well?'

The alien nodded enthusiastically.

'I'll explain everything when we're together. I promise I'll be gentle with you – at first'.

Charlie attempted to look brave. 'No pain, no gain', he replied and whisked himself out of the room.

A silence fell as the door closed behind the little alien.

Bruno stood rigid, unable to relax. He had assumed a leadership role and made an important decision. Even though the fear still chipped away at his confidence, Bruno felt empowered.

Granddad regarded the boy with interest; he swelled with pride. He could not believe how quickly Bruno not only adapted to his surroundings but proved to be a fighter, a leader. This boy was fast becoming a man.

CHAPTER 12

SOLIDARITY

Having arrived early, Bruno paced the stage of the amphitheatre. He waited eagerly for the others and wondered how they would react to his plan. He knew Summer would support him and so would Charlie, who in turn would convince the other aliens. However, he had to have Carlos and Elzbieta on his side as well if his plan had any chance of working.

Summer excitedly bounded into the room. Her hair had been pulled back into a tight ponytail that swished from side to side as she ran down the stairs. Her contagious smile caused his spirits to soar.

'Bruno!' she chirped happily, landing with a jump just in front of him. 'So what's the plan?' She looked up at him with such adoration that Bruno found it hard to resist telling her what he had in mind.

Instead he circled his arms around her and lightly kissed her nose. 'All in good time. I need everyone together'.

Summer was about to respond to this when the door opened again. Charlie led the other five aliens into the room, all of whom were buzzing excitedly and chattering non-stop. Together they descended the stairs with their usual grace. Charlie acknowledged Bruno with a quick wave and grinned widely, as though he had completed an important task. Following them was Carlos and Elzbieta, although they stepped in more cautiously, almost suspicious as to why they were asked to be present at this meeting.

Bruno waited until everyone had settled in the front row seats. He a clear divide between the aliens and the humans as they placed themselves into two groups. The aliens sat on the left and the humans on the right, with one empty seat between them.

When he finally got everyone's attention, he began. 'As you are aware, we need to work together as a team in order to survive. For some time, we have been living under the same roof, working together and eating together. There has been so much talk about unity and the need to battle as one'. He paused dramatically, savouring the fact that he had captured his audience. 'Look at how you're sitting'. Again he paused for effect. 'Do we look united? Do we look as though we can fight as one?'

His audience looked at each other, some bending forward to see the whole row. A whispered confusion ensued.

'If we're to show togetherness, we need to start by sitting together'.

Slowly, timidly, Charlie rose from his seat, glancing around at the others. With a serious expression, he stepped forward and walked towards the right-hand side. He reached Carlos and smiled at him. Carlos, clearly not enjoying being picked as well as now becoming the focus of attention, raised himself from his seat. He started to move towards the left-hand side as Charlie sat in the vacated seat. The others watched this intently, and then, en mass, got out of their seats and arranged themselves so that human sat next to alien. The atmosphere lightened as a few giggles could be heard.

Bruno smiled. 'It's clear that training will have to be far more intense and not just because of the announcement yesterday. Elzbieta, you will teach the person on your left how to fight; Carlos, the same for you. Summer and I will teach two people each. We will not only teach you to defend yourselves but to get to know you well. We need to build solidarity. Yesterday I watched as different human races dined together peacefully. Now I want humans and aliens to be true allies against the enemy. Once you're ready, you will join us to teach others until everyone can make a stand against the Gwarks'.

As Bruno mentioned the name, the aliens whimpered and cowered.

'Before long, the mention of Gwarks will not fill you with fear but a need to defeat them, charged with anger and the secure knowledge that we can do this together'.

There was a stunned silence. Bruno looked at his audience. He had hoped for a round of applause and exultant cheers. All he got was a row of open-mouthed statues. He let the silence remain as he could not think of anything else to add.

Suddenly Summer shouted, 'To solidarity! To Bruno!' and this seemed to wake the rest of them. They all joined in calling out the very same words.

As the aliens made their way out of the hall with instructions of where and when to meet their teachers, Bruno turned his attention to Summer. 'I think that went well?'

'Bruno, that was amazing'. Summer beamed at him, and Bruno basked in her compliment.

CHAPTER 13

THE LESSONS BEGIN

AFTER A LIGHT lunch, the aliens met with their teachers in different locations around the great hall. Bruno decided to meet Charlie and another alien in the amphitheatre. All three gathered on the stage; it was clear that the two aliens, although terrified of getting hurt, were eager to learn. They stared at Bruno in wide-eyed wonder, waiting for instructions.

Bruno commenced with the pleasantries. 'Charlie, who have you brought with you?' He smiled, trying to put them at ease.

Charlie stepped forward slightly. 'This is my best friend'.

His friend was looking down and nervously shuffling his feet.

Bruno turned to him and attempted to use a friendly yet authoritative tone. 'What's your name?'

The alien opened his mouth and let out high-pitched squeals that caused Bruno to clasp his hands tightly against his ears. After the alien finished, he looked up at Bruno with an expression of astonishment as Bruno stared at him blankly. The alien swept his head towards Charlie, who found the whole situation so amusing that he chuckled uncontrollably. He held his hands over his mouth, preventing the chuckles from turning into laughter. His face had turned pink from the strain, and his shoulders shook.

'Your Granddad gave us names that he could pronounce', Charlie managed once he had more control over himself. 'This is Tim'.

Tim beamed and frantically nodded. 'Yes, I am Tim. Sorry; in my excitement I forgot to use my human name'.

'Please don't apologize', Bruno answered quickly. 'I find your language fascinating. I just don't think my voice could cope with the pitch or the sounds'.

The conversation soon turned to more pressing matters. Bruno told Tim to take a seat while he wanted to teach Charlie some basic moves. 'This time we will take things a little bit slower', he assured Charlie, who was already quivering.

After half an hour, Bruno felt Charlie was ready to try out the moves. 'Okay, remember what I just showed you. Block any punches I throw, and then move in for the attack. Keep your fists clenched, thumbs tucked in front of the fingers so they don't break with the impact'.

Charlie squatted and bounced up and down slightly, ready to anticipate any movement from his opponent. He set his face into a serious and menacing expression; his eyes narrowed and his lips became hard lines. This time he held his fists up, ready to cover his face or block any blow that came towards him.

Bruno could not help but be impressed with the transformation. Stepping forward, Bruno adjusted his own position so he too was ready to fight.

In the front row, Tim was glued to the stage, jumping up and down with excitement. The atmosphere became electric, tension permeating from the three of them. After a brief pause, both opponents sized each other up, and Bruno lunged.

Quick as a snake, Charlie backed away, using his powers to elevate for a moment before making contact with the ground once more. The motion was so fluid and extremely quick that Bruno was unsure of what he had just witnessed. Every punch Bruno threw was either blocked by an arm, a leg, or simply by moving to another spot beside or even behind Bruno. Every time he focused on the alien, he was faced with the same cheerful grin that made him all the more agitated. The alien showed no signs of tiring or breaking out in a sweat.

After some time, Bruno stopped. He bent over, hands on his knees, and panted.

The alien stood upright, hands dangling at his sides once more. 'How did I do?' he asked, although Bruno detected an air of confidence in his tone of voice.

'You know you did well …at dodging. You still need to learn how to attack. Yes, you are doing so much better'. Bruno regained his breath and his heart was no longer thumping furiously in his chest.

He wiped the sweat from his brow and rubbed his hand on his head. 'I didn't know you could be so quick and could levitate, Charlie. That would be very useful in battle'. After a moment, he asked, 'Are you all so light-footed and quick?'

Charlie nodded and looked towards Tim. Tim merely glanced at Charlie and gave a quick nod. Within the blink of an eye he stood in front of Bruno wearing the same cheerful grin as his friend.

Bruno jumped back in surprise, and for a moment was speechless. 'I wish I could do that', he whispered, mostly to himself.

'I'm sure that could be arranged', Tim replied, but Bruno barely registered this.

With great enthusiasm, Bruno babbled, 'The Gwarks are heavy and slow beings, right? Well, there's an advantage to being full of speed, and with your abilities, you will easily confuse them. We must build on these talents that you possess. Tim, go and get the others. I have an idea'.

Tim left the room without question, and Charlie sat down, patiently waiting for Bruno to explain himself.

It didn't take long until the whole group was together.

Bruno stood once more before them. 'I want to show you something'. This was all he said and gestured for Charlie to join him onstage.

He turned to Elzbieta and said, 'You too'.

Elzbieta frowned at him but nevertheless obeyed his command.

'Elzbieta and Charlie will now fight', he announced proudly, causing the audience to murmur phrases of concern and confusion.

Elzbieta's frown deepened, and her eyes bore into Bruno.

'Trust me, Elzbieta', he whispered, placing his hand on her shoulder. 'Charlie, show them what you showed me'.

Again Charlie prepared to get ready to stand in his fighting position, but this time he attempted an even more menacing expression.

Elzbieta raised her eyebrows and prepared herself.

It all started well as Charlie ducked and dived, floated over her, and at one time even flipped over in slow motion with such elaborate sophistication that the audience applauded. Elzbieta was left rather dizzy as he continuously spun around her. The crowd went wild as Charlie's confidence mounted. After every move he cheerfully grinned, which irritated Elzbieta as much as it did Bruno. He also bowed to the audience dramatically; it was clear he enjoyed the attention he was receiving and was getting rather carried away with the whole show.

As he swiftly turned to Elzbieta, she punched him hard on the face. He tumbled back and fell to the floor, stunned. When his vision began to clear, he looked up at Elzbieta, who smiled down at him.

'That wiped the smile off your face', she said with great satisfaction. 'Never get too confident, never take your eye off your opponent, and most of all, never underestimate a woman!'

Charlie whimpered softly and held his nose.

Bruno, lost for words, stared at the scene. Suddenly all of the aliens rushed forward to comfort their friend, who remained on the floor complaining about the pain. Large globes of tears gushed from his eyes as he wailed uncontrollably.

'Elzbieta, come here now!' he ordered.

Elzbieta marched towards him, her expression hard. Even though she showed such aggression, her delicate poise never faltered.

'What do you think you're doing? We're supposed to build their confidence, not brutalize them. Look at the poor thing'. Bruno surveyed the scene again. Charlie had managed to sit up by now and snivelled silently. The other aliens were still showing concern and circled around him with soothing words.

Elzbieta exclaimed, 'Yes, look at him. Do you think I enjoyed hurting him? What he was doing a moment ago was ballet dancing, not fighting. He did not make any attempt to attack. This is not a game, Bruno, this is war. What would he do in battle? He would curl up and cry if someone pushed him over. The aliens must toughen up. It will be violent and bloodthirsty; many will die. We are all frightened, Bruno, but we must show courage in order to survive'.

Bruno stared at the waif-like flower before him and could not believe the strength that was encased in her frail frame. Deep down he knew she was right, but it seemed so cruel.

Again he gathered everyone. 'Charlie, it may have hurt, but you will get used to it'.

He then spoke to everyone. 'Remember, the Gwarks will not be so considerate. Weakness shall not be tolerated, as weakness will mean death in battle. We must all fight our fears before we fight our enemy. Today Charlie has shown us a special skill that you all possess. We will use this skill as a basis for your training. Obviously defending yourselves is not an issue, but attack is. We will start again tomorrow'.

Elzbieta smiled at Bruno.

CHAPTER 14

STANDING ON THE SHOULDERS OF GIANTS

THAT EVENING, BRUNO recounted the day to Granddad, who listened silently. On occasions between sipping his drink, he nodded, smiled, or merely shook his head in disbelief. The events poured out easily for Bruno, and with them his concerns and lack of self-belief.

'Bruno, you've come a long way. I'm so proud of you. Your courage and constant reassessing of the situation before you proves what a great leader you will be'. The old man leaned towards the boy, giving him the magical comfort that only a true grandparent can give.

'I didn't ask to be a leader', Bruno lamented, reaching for the old man's hand. 'What should I do?'

Granddad grasped Bruno's hand tightly in his own. 'So you want to know where to go from here. The aliens have no knowledge of violence; they have never witnessed a man taking the life of another, not for real in front of their eyes. For them, death has no pain; they make sure of that, and it is dealt with respectfully and calmly. You must give them the experience of the violent side of death – the gore, the pain, and the stomach-clenching fear that will grip them. Use your imagination, boy'.

Bruno thought deeply about this, and Granddad had the patience to remain quiet, allowing him time to consider a way forward. He leaned back in his chair, letting go of the boy's hand, and continued to sip his drink.

After some thought, Bruno said, 'I could ask your friend to run a documentary or a film movie that we have about war. Lots of them are very realistic'.

'Harry would be able to do that. Yes, that's a good start. And then what?'

Before long, a strategy was devised, and both were satisfied the plan was a good one.

'I'll talk to Harry and organise the showing of the documentary. I'll also explain the relevance of your actions and how important it is for everyone to cooperate with your requests. I personally see no alternative plan'. Granddad sighed heavily. He was so tired, and the pain in his back was getting worse. However, the thought of being part of such an important decision kept him going. 'I'll see him in a moment – the sooner the better'.

Bruno smiled. 'I couldn't have done anything like this without you. Thanks'. He paused before adding, 'I think you're amazing'.

Granddad's face lit up, and he sat up with sudden energy; he could see it in Bruno's face and by the tone of his voice that he sincerely meant this. 'You have given me a purpose, and in all honesty I believe you are the grandson I should have had'.

Granddad slowly clambered to his feet. 'I'll see Harry now, and you need to sleep. You have a big day ahead of you tomorrow'. He toddled towards the door and left without another word.

Bruno thought it would be impossible to sleep, as there was so much to think about. But before he knew it, he fell into a deep slumber.

CHAPTER 15

BRUTAL TRUTHS

THE ALARM SOUNDED throughout the whole building. It bellowed loudly, slicing through the corridors and disturbing the peaceful dreams of the many sleepers. Calm, composed, crevasse-free faces became aging frowns. Fear and worry taunted each waking person like ice picks, creating furrows of stress on each brow. Blissful tranquillity was shattered as a riot of activity ensued. Pattering of feet escalated into a thunderous charge, and energetic whispers surged into an intense avalanche. Bodies torpedoed in and out of rooms, creating a hazardous display of frantic dancing, colliding with each other as arms and legs erratically waved in the air. Each person had a place to be, yet with panic, a whirlwind of fumbling caused progress to be slow.

Bruno listened to the wail of the alarm and stood as firm as a statue. His fists were clenched, and the blood pulsed with adrenaline, firing oxygen to his brain. He had never felt so clearheaded as he did at that moment. Eyes shining like the beacon of a lighthouse, he waited for his troops to arrive. Bruno had made all the necessary preparations for the day.

Trickling into the amphitheatre, the aliens gathered shoal-like; huddled together with wide-eyed wonder, they waited. Elzbieta and Carlos stood quietly at the side, observing the scene before them.

'Are you sure you're ready for this?' Summer whispered into Bruno's ear whilst placing a reassuring hand on his shoulder.

'Do I have a choice?' His sharp response revealed how exposed he felt. After a brief pause, he looked into Summer's imploring eyes and smiled in an attempt to appease her.

After taking a deep breath, Bruno began. 'We know war is inevitable. We know we must stand our ground and fight. However, I believe you are not ready for it. Yes, you have great skills, which will be useful, but at this point, you will not survive the cold, hard realities of war. There will be pain, bloodshed, and death'.

Bruno paused to gage the audience's reaction to his words. The atmosphere thickened into a solidifying liquid. He could almost smell the trepidation as it spread amongst the listeners. He decided not to take his speech too far in fear that it would have the wrong effect. He wanted to make them aware of their weakness and not cause them to surrender to their cowardice.

'Today we will start by educating you about the realities of war'. He nodded to Charlie, who had been absorbing every word that left Bruno's mouth.

With a quick nod back, Charlie clicked his fingers and a huge white sheet of plastic fell in slow and controlled motion from above until it hung proudly, suspended before them. As the lights dimmed, everyone took a seat.

The music set the tone of the documentary with disturbing clarity. Violins cried, drums trembled, and the piano spoke of pain and suffering. A clarinet wailed, calling for hope, but was drowned by the clatter of symbols that smashed everything else into submission. Shock, bewilderment, and sorrow swept through the room as images of brutality and torment were cruelly displayed. Gore and pain were played out in equal measures, as though Satan himself choreographed each move. Some of the aliens wept hysterically; others stared blankly, unable to fully take in what they were seeing. A few fainted.

Finally the lights came back on and the screen returned to its hiding place, but the heavy cloak of silence remained. Silent sobs perforated the air.

Elzbieta sniffed discreetly and wiped her eyes. Seeing this, Carlos put his arm around her but quickly retreated as his advances were rejected. Summer found Bruno's hand and held it tightly. Her eyes shined wildly, red-rimmed with evidence of heartfelt tears tracing the contours of her cheeks.

Bruno swallowed hard, trying to ease the lump that had formed in his throat. With a cracked voice he managed, 'Fifteen-minute break. Meet in the dining hall'.

As the aliens plodded away, Bruno carefully watched them.

Charlie turned back towards him, lips quivering and eyes filled like lakes over-spilling their banks. The expression on his face pained Bruno as he scowled accusingly. His whole demeanour communicated the hurt and sorrow he felt from watching the documentary.

The pain deepened when Charlie mouthed the words, 'How could you?' and then turned away to catch up with the other aliens who were leaving the room.

'They'll get over it', Elzbieta commented.

'I hope so'. Bruno whispered. 'I truly hope so'.

Chapter 16

TRAINING BEGINS

AFTER A VERY subdued fifteen minutes, the aliens filed into the dining hall. Even though their mood had not lightened much, Bruno was pleased to see they had not completely given up on him. Charlie even managed a brief smile before lowering his head. Bruno moved towards him – slowly, careful not to scare him – and patted him on the back.

Charlie stared straight into Bruno's eyes and his feelings of adoration flooded his face. 'I trust you'.

'I only want to help you, not hurt you', Bruno replied.

Charlie's smile broadened. To Bruno the smile resembled the sun shining through dark clouds.

'Well, what's next?' Charlie asked eagerly. The determination and willingness to please had returned.

Each alien was given a sword. Even though they were warned how sharp the instruments were, most managed to cut themselves. Summer, Elzbieta, and Carlos helped the aliens hold their swords correctly while Bruno gave orders from the front of the room. Twelve bulging sacks hung in a neat row. Others waited, lined up against the side of the room. Only Bruno, Granddad, and one of the chefs knew what was in them. Whenever Elzbieta looked at those sacks with a puzzled expression, Bruno laughed.

He was not surprised to see Granddad shuffle into the room, and as he approached, he smiled cheekily at Bruno. 'Here to watch the show?' Bruno remarked humorously.

'Wouldn't miss this for the world, my dear boy'. Granddad grinned.

Twelve of the aliens were instructed to stand on the opposite side of the room and face the sacks. All they had to do was run towards their target and push their swords through them.

'Surely this is pointless', Carlos grumbled. 'The enemy will not just stand still'.

'Be quiet, Carlos', Elzbieta berated. 'I think Bruno is up to something. Those sacks look a bit suspicious to me'.

'Oh no, not another one of his strange plans', Carlos moaned.

Summer gave him a scolding glance that made him be quiet.

The aliens clumsily held their swords in front of themselves; their faces were screwed up with concentration. On Bruno's signal, they charged towards the sacks and plunged their swords into the heart of each one. On impact, the sacks exploded, spraying the aliens with warm red liquid. The floor was soaked, making the surface slippery. Cries of sheer panic filled the hall as the aliens flapped their arms and legs in an attempt to remain standing. Those watching ran towards them with distressed faces and open arms, but stopped at the edge of the red surface. Some reached forward, but none of them wanted to step in the liquid. The aliens that were now drenched screamed wildly, frantically touching their bodies as if looking for wounds.

Granddad laughed heartily and clapped his hands. 'Well done, Bruno! What a display'.

Bruno beamed and looked towards Summer, who still appeared shocked. Carlos and Elzbieta giggled uncontrollably and were explaining something to her.

'What did you decide to use in the end?' Granddad asked curiously. 'It looks very realistic'.

'Just watered-down ketchup'. He too was surprised at how well it turned out. 'I'd better put them out of their misery'.

With this he called for silence; however, the aliens were not so responsive this time, and it took several moments before a sense of order had been restored. After explaining that no one was hurt and that the substance was in fact edible and not dangerous, Bruno ordered for more sacks to be put in place. It was important to continue because in battle, no-one would clear up the blood for them. Bruno wanted it to be as messy and gory as possible.

For the next hour, the aliens sank their swords into sacks, getting more and more soaked. Even though they no longer screamed, it was still obvious they did not enjoy the experience. Whimpers could be heard as each sack released its contents.

Exhausted, the aliens pleaded for a break, but Bruno refused until the last sack had been burst. A half-hearted cheer echoed around the room once this had been done, and the aliens sauntered away to wash and change their clothes. An early lunch was not granted as Bruno insisted they complete one more task before they ate.

'Are you not being a bit harsh?' Granddad warned.

'Granddad, you know they're ready for the next stage. It would be better to do it on empty stomachs'. Bruno raised his eyebrow and grimaced. Even he was not looking forward to the next task, so he was keenly aware how it would affect the squeamish aliens.

Granddad understood and replied. 'I think I'll stay out of the next one. Good luck, my boy; you're doing so well'. He winked at Bruno and slowly made his way towards the door.

Bruno noticed he was hunched over further than before and rubbed his leg more often. Granddad was quickly weakening, and Bruno was concerned.

'Rest up now', he called after Granddad. 'I'll let you know later how it went'.

Granddad continued his journey towards their room and waved to acknowledge he'd heard Bruno.

Summer slipped her hand under Bruno's arm and tightened her grip. Gaining his attention, she rested her head on the arm she held on to. 'I'm tired. Let's sit down for a while'.

'Yes, good idea. I'm thirsty'. Bruno kissed the top of her head and together they moved out of the room.

Elzbieta and Carlos followed behind, leaving the mess they had all made.

Chapter 17

PUSHED TOO FAR

Elzbieta sat heavily in the armchair and cupped a glass of water in her hands. Slowly she sipped and revelled in the coolness of the liquid as it slid down her throat. The sensation radiated around her body, and as it rejuvenated her, she sank deeper into the seat. It had been a tiring day both emotionally and physically. The last task before lunch had pushed everyone to the limit. She closed her eyes and surrendered to her deepest thoughts; she had let herself down. Her mother had always brought her up to be tough and strong minded so that she could face any difficulties that life could possibly throw at her. Most of her family had battled the cruellest experiences: starvation, illness, abuse, war, and the death of loved ones. All of them came through every situation with determination and dignity and, in fact, praised the Lord above that things weren't worse.

'And what did I go and do?' she whispered sternly to herself. In her mind, she replayed the events that would shame her for the rest of her life. She could see the pig's head resting on the table in front of her and a sharp kitchen knife lying beside it. She could smell the nauseating stench of blood, its metallic odour creeping up her nostrils until it filled them to capacity. Beads of sweat had broken out on her forehead, and she'd begun to feel light-headed. Everyone was watching her.

With shaking hands she'd grasped the knife and lifted it in the air where it wavered uncontrollably. She looked at the pig, which appeared to be smirking at her. Its grey tongue had flopped to the side of its mouth, and its eyes stared at her with intensity, daring her to make her move. She wanted to rip her eyes away from the wretched thing but was held transfixed. She could even see the bristles on its face, its skin like leather.

The room was strangely silent, as though her audience was waiting for her next move. She'd moved the knife towards the head, and spots danced in front of her eyes. The light faded, and the sweat turned to droplets that ran down her face. Then there was nothing but darkness. Elzbieta had fainted.

'How humiliating', she said with a moan. She was just glad she was not wearing a dress and hoped her fall had been graceful. 'I hope I didn't pull a funny face'.

'You looked beautiful'. Carlos had walked in and caught the last few words.

Elzbieta was startled and jumped, opening her eyes quickly to see who had interrupted her thoughts. 'Can't you just leave me alone?' she whined, perturbed.

Carlos tried to reassure her. 'Stop beating yourself up about it. I thought you were brave to volunteer in the first place. If it was me, I would have puked up all over the place'.

'Yes, well, if I had done that, I would've had to kill myself', she mumbled.

Carlos gave a fake laugh, but looking at her expression, was not sure she didn't really mean it. 'There is no shame in being sensitive. For goodness sake, you're human, you know. I actually like that side of you – strong but still in need of a man to look after you'. Kneeling beside her he grinned and winked at her.

Rolling her eyes, Elzbieta lightly slapped his arm. She knew he adored her, but the feeling was not mutual. Her heart had settled on Bruno, and it hurt to know he only had eyes for Summer. Due to this, she returned Carlos's affections with friendship and promised to always be good to him.

'Did you see what Tim did? You know, Charlie's friend?' Carlos tried to lighten the mood. He was pleased to see a smile appear on her face. He had never seen such a beautiful girl as her. Like an angel, she was his guiding light. When he was near her, nothing else mattered, and everything else faded into insignificance. She was his strength, his hope, his life; she owned his soul.

Elzbieta answered, 'Yes, what a silly little alien'. Her smile broadened with the memory. 'It was sweet though. I wondered what was going on when he started to stroke the rabbit and talk to it. He really believed he had killed it by stroking it too hard. He didn't realise it was already dead'.

'Well, I really am a bit scared of Bruno sometimes', Carlos confided. 'His ideas are a bit freaky. Even I felt woozy at the sight of all those carcasses. Making the aliens carve them up was absolutely horrible. Where did he get that idea?'

Elzbieta became defensive. 'He's only trying to toughen them up. It was effective and will help them when they have to fight'.

This was noticed by Carlos, but he chose to let it go. 'I killed the rabbit; I am a murderer!' He copied Tim's high-pitched tone.

They laughed, and it felt so good. Once they gained control of themselves, they fell into a thoughtful silence.

'Do you think we will be able to really do this?' Elzbieta questioned with clear uncertainty.

'We'd better. I don't like the thought of the alternative'. With that, Carlos gently put his arm around her shoulder, and Elzbieta accepted it.

Chapter 18

A LITTLE FAITH

BRUNO HAD SLEPT soundly the whole night through. The need to recharge his batteries was extremely important as he had another jam-packed day planned. In order for the aliens to be ready for battle, a lot of work still needed to be done. Dozing warmly, he allowed his whole body to relax. The aches and pains of yesterday were numbed by rest. However, any movement would see them resurrected and claw in revenge up and down every muscle in his body.

'Bruno. Bruno, wake up'.

From a distance someone was calling him.

'Bruno, Bruno!'

This time hands shoved against his back, causing his limp body to shake back and forth. Frowning, he moaned and became rigid, holding himself in place as well as stretching his tired tendons. His eyes felt glued together, and it took incredible force to separate them. Confused, he summoned every ounce of energy to surface the boundaries of sleep; squinting, he focused on the face before him.

Granddad, already dressed and ready for the day ahead, smiled down at him. Bruno could not help but notice that, as always, he smelt freshly washed and his hair was neatly placed. Did he ever sleep?

'Ah! He wakes', the old man commented, his voice melodic with the joy of life. 'Harry has requested your presence. It must be important. Quickly, sort yourself out. Brush your hair and clean up'.

Grumbling furiously under his breath, Bruno emerged from beneath the quilt and tumbled out of bed.

'Now who's the old man?' Granddad chortled and smiled broadly at the boy. 'I personally feel very refreshed. For once I can move with not even a twinge'.

Bruno studied the old man, and even though his movements were sharper and his face more radiant than usual, he suspected Granddad was clinging to any sense of strength he had left. The dark circles still hung below his eyes, and his hand twitched involuntarily from time to time.

Forcing him into action military style, Granddad made sure Bruno was dressed and out the door. Keeping to the pace set for him, Bruno marched down the corridor towards the great hall, where he was to meet Harry. All was silent as most of the people were still asleep. Bruno envied them as he passed each closed door.

Harry was waiting rather impatiently at the entrance and paced from side to side. His agitation fuelled the other aliens around him with nervousness. Each set of eyes followed his every movement but no one dared utter a word.

When Bruno emerged from behind the door, attention was diverted to him. In an attempt to appear composed, Harry stiffened, straightening his back, giving him an air of superiority. Fidgeting hands were clasped behind his back, yet he spoke with ease. 'Bruno, thank you for coming so quickly. Please follow me'.

Harry swiftly turned, moved towards the back of the room, and walked through yet another door.

Bruno had not entered this room before so was curious to see what it was like. The lighting was softened for a more calming effect, and the walls were painted soft peach, which imposed a relaxed atmosphere. The floor was smooth, rich oak panels that glowed with health. It was obvious that it was well maintained. The desk was simple yet expensively solid. The chair behind the desk was huge and appeared to be made from soft leather. There was a subtle aroma of new furniture, and Bruno wondered how often Harry actually occupied this space. There was no scrunched-up paper in the bin, and the pencils stood to attention in the jar, all sharpened. Harry settled in the huge chair and immediately became engulfed by it. Bruno reached for the smaller chair placed by the side wall and pulled it towards the front of the desk. Facing each other, they waited for the right moment to speak.

Bruno was about to open his mouth to start the conversation when Harry put a single finger to his lips. Just at that moment the alarm sounded, signifying the start of another day. Bruno had grown accustomed to its sound and no longer flinched. Once it reached its peak, it stopped, leaving the sensation of ringing in his ears. Bruno was no longer affected by this.

It was clear Harry would begin. 'So I hear training has gone very well so far'.

'Yes it has, better than I could have imagined. They are very keen'. Bruno answered quickly.

'Good, good'.

There was an uncomfortable pause.

'Harry, sir', Bruno started, 'why did you ask me here? I mean, I don't think you want to know how things are going as you already have that information'.

Harry smiled and nodded at Bruno's perceptiveness. 'That is true. I must admit though, I am struggling to find a way of introducing the topic to you. I do not know how you will react to my request'.

Bruno laughed nervously. 'Ever since arriving here, all I've had are strange requests and bizarre experiences. I don't think anything else will really surprise me now. Just cut to the chase. What is it?'

'As you wish'. The alien responded. Adjusting his position in the chair, he began. 'I'm amazed at how you have taken on the task of preparing us to fight against the Gwarks. Your commitment to our cause has been overwhelming. However, I am sure you are fully aware of the fact that, given the short amount of time we have, no matter what you do, we will never truly be ready to match our enemy's strength and ability. Please do not think I have no faith in you or my men. I am just being honest with you – and myself, for that matter'.

'They have improved so much', Bruno muttered despondently.

'I do not deny that, and these improvements will be very necessary when the time comes. At least now we have an army of enthusiastic soldiers who believe in themselves. If not for you, we would not have had that. There is another request to make of you. If we are to have any chance of survival, you must lead our army'. Harry paused to allow Bruno time to digest what was asked of him.

Quietly Bruno repeated, 'Lead the army'. So many thoughts raced into his mind: travelling into space, using laser guns, being on another planet, meeting the dreaded Gwarks. Fear struck like a panther, carefully pawing at the pride and excitement that dominated the very core of his emotions. He was chosen to be the leader, the courageous hero, and the adventure would be challenging – but what an experience! How could he not accept? After everything he had already been through, declining would be absurd. Pride and excitement roared like a lion and the panther darted off, beaten. Strangely, he realised that he cared for the aliens and had considered himself to be part of their lives. He was not a prisoner but someone who they respected and treated as an equal. He was no longer Bruno, the ordinary boy at school but something much more. Also, as Summer had pointed out, he was blanked out from his parents' memory. If he helped the aliens then he was sure that they would take him back home and remove the spell that they had put on his family. Besides, he felt the need to make Granddad proud. Granddad was not just a companion to whom he clung but a very special person in his life. He was now 'his' Granddad. As Bruno considered all of this, he found it frightening just how much trust he had put in these alien beings. However, he had no choice.

'I will lead your army', Bruno responded eagerly.

'Granddad, as you call him, was so right about you. We've had many conversations which were dominated by his praise for you'. Harry clapped joyfully.

At the mention of Granddad, Bruno's thoughts swayed to a more important subject. 'Is there nothing you can do for him?' His tone became lower, more intense. His eyes began to sting with tears and his voice wavered. 'You must see how he's fading'.

Harry's expression saddened as though already considering a great loss. Bowing his head, he exhaled slowly. 'Bruno, his end is near. What am I supposed to do about that?'

Becoming more frustrated, Bruno raised his voice. 'I've seen what you can do. All those experiments you do in the great hall, all the abilities you possess, surely you can heal him. You took him from the hands of death before and you can do it again'. Suddenly Bruno burst into tears and howled uncontrollably.

Harry observed this and waited until Bruno could contain himself. Harry spoke soothingly. 'Bruno, when it is time, there is nothing anyone can do. When we took Granddad from the home, it was his fate to be chosen. We could have taken the woman in the next room or the man in the room above. In fact, we could have decided to go to another home altogether. Out of all the people that we could have taken, it was by divine intervention that we prolonged his life. I will not accept any responsibility for this, as it was God's will. It was not his time to go, as his purpose on earth had not been completely fulfilled. God gives and God takes away; no one has the right to question his decisions. In my opinion, Granddad had to meet you. Now you have to be strong and let him go. Remember this: in death, he will find peace and be with his wife. It is those who remain behind who suffer. Be grateful that you had time with him; his love for you and faith in you is a great gift. Hold on to the memories you have, and strive to always make him proud. He will always be with you in your heart'.

Bruno blinked back the tears and sniffed. 'He isn't dead yet'.

'Yes, so embrace every moment you have with him and stop complaining'. Harry ordered. 'Talking of wasting time, let's move on. There's another part to my request'.

Bruno could see Harry's eyes were moist. Granddad had touched more than one life; maybe he had more than one purpose on Earth.

CHAPTER 19

THE PILL

HARRY PRESSED A button on the side of his desk whilst Bruno solemnly wiped his eyes. Both waited in silence, deep in their own thoughts. Bruno could not help but wonder what the alien had in store for him – as if the amazing thought of him leading an army was not enough.

The door suddenly swished open, and an alien carrying a clipboard entered the room. Bruno had not yet met this one and became curious as to how many of their race actually inhabited the underground building. This alien promptly advanced towards the desk and looked towards Harry for further instructions. He appeared far more confident and acted as Harry's equal. So far, he did not even glance at Bruno, which made the boy feel suddenly inferior. He stood straight, unmoving, as if to conserve all energy for matters of importance.

'Explain the procedure of transformation to Bruno please', Harry commanded.

The alien turned his head sharply towards Harry, and his expression changed to disbelief and horror. 'But this is top-secret information withheld from the humans. This was discussed only recently. Knowledge of such a thing could put us in danger'. Leaning forward, he whispered, 'The humans cannot be trusted'. With this he finally glanced at Bruno, the distrust evident on his face.

'And are we not already in danger?' Harry raised his voice out of frustration. 'Bruno is on our side and needs to know. He will need it before long'.

The other alien gawped at Harry, shocked. 'The boy?' was all he could say. His head swung at Bruno and then back at Harry.

Harry looked at the other alien sternly, which prompted him into doing as he was instructed.

Using the tone of a professional scientist, he began. 'We have created a way of transforming the human body into any required shape and form. Once dispersed through the system, the liquid will run through the bloodstream, affecting each cell and weakening the bone structure. Once this has been achieved, the bones are manipulated before they reform into the predetermined shape. Internal organs change in size in order to fit into the new form. Once completed, the original body is unrecognisable. It is a remarkable and fascinating invention. The only drawback is that it is a very painful process. Nothing can be done about that'.

Bruno was completely mystified by what he had just heard, but he was also terrified by the idea that this was part of Harry's request.

'How does this involve me?' Bruno's voice became a high-pitched whine.

Harry replied, 'As you know, you're going to lead the army against the Gwarks. However, your human form is in many ways inferior to ours. You have seen what physical skills we have, and this would be very beneficial to you. The combination of your abilities fused with ours would make you almost invincible'.

'So what does this involve? Are you going to inject me with a slimy liquid and then force my body into different positions?' Bruno asked nervously.

'Don't be absurd', the scientist said. 'It's a pill that you consume orally. The rest happens by itself in fewer than fifty seconds'.

The memory of the nightmare came flooding back into Bruno's mind. The way he howled excitedly in battle, his face turning into a wide grin, showing sharp, pointed teeth. The face melting and moulding into something inhuman, changing into an alien himself. He shivered.

Harry continued. 'When you get into battle, you will take one of these pills, and straightaway you will transform'.

The scientist cut in, 'It lasts for perhaps five hours. Then your body should return to its former shape. We have not managed to test it on anyone yet, but the theory is airtight'.

'Great, I'm a guinea pig', Bruno whispered.

The two aliens exchanged confused glances.

'You will not change into an animal, just be one of us for a while. The pill will be made especially for you', the scientist explained innocently.

'Looks like I don't have any choice – yet again'.

This satisfied Harry, and he grinned contently.

Chapter 20

TIME TO THINK

Rolling the glass between his palms, Bruno stared at the liquid sloshing to and fro. The rhythm of his movements caused the lemonade to swirl and bubble close to the rim. Bruno stared but hardly noticed as his mind was clogged with all kinds of thoughts and emotions. Would the pill work? Would he return to himself afterwards? He did not like the words used by the scientist; 'probably', 'should', and 'theory' were not comforting. The idea of fifty seconds of absolute pain alarmed him. Fifty seconds did not sound like a lot when the activity was enjoyable or even mundane but in agony would seem like forever. He brought the glass to his mouth and paused. He was not thirsty and did not want to drink. He looked at the gassy spray that clung to the side of the glass and then placed it on the stage beside him.

The door slammed and a quick tapping of footsteps were heard, pelting down the stairs towards him. Bruno did not bother to see who it was.

'I thought I would find you here'. Elzbieta's soothing voice stirred a feeling of calm, unravelling the knots in his stomach. 'You practically live here'.

She sat next to him on the stage. Bruno felt her presence and smiled when he noticed she sat close enough to show interest in his thoughts but far enough not to be overbearing.

Both remained silent. Elzbieta showed such patience that Bruno sensed no agitation. Her breathing was quiet and slow, and she sat unmoving, relaxed. 'I like it here. It's so quiet, especially at this time of day'.

Bruno aid, 'This is where I was reunited with Summer. If it wasn't for the aliens taking me, I suppose I wouldn't have ever seen her again. Strange isn't it? Life I mean'.

Elzbieta glanced at him and offered an awkward smile. 'Yes, it's strange. We all wouldn't have met if it wasn't for this'. Hoping to gently probe Bruno into opening up to her, she commented, 'You spent a long time talking to Harry earlier'.

Bruno smirked and laughed quietly. 'Not much gets past you, does it?' Growing more serious he added, 'Yes, I suppose I was'. Then, in great detail, everything that was said, every thought he'd had, and every emotion he ever felt tumbled furiously from his mouth. Once he began, he couldn't stop, and Elzbieta just listened.

Bruno came to an abrupt end and bowed his head. The experiences and emotions were such a burden on his young shoulders, and the effects were starting to surface. He bore the expression of a man in the latter years of his life. However, the fear and need for comfort still showed that his youth and inexperience was predominant.

He leaned towards Elzbieta, and without a word, she embraced him in her arms with the warmth and care of a mother hoping to shelter her child from the cruel world. For some time they remained this way. The feelings expressed by the tableau would have melted the coldest heart and give hope to the very hopeless and be proof that in a world of hate, love shines like a beacon on the hilltops.

'Am I interrupting?' Summer's harsh tone shattered the serene atmosphere, and the two friends broke away.

'I was just being there for him', Elzbieta said. Even though her heated face gave away her embarrassment, her voice remained calm.

'I can see that'. Summer's reply was tainted with sarcasm. Her eyes bore into Elzbieta's but lowered in defeat as her contender refused to relent. Before another word could be said, Elzbieta excused herself and left. There was no point in causing trouble; there were more important matters to deal with.

Bruno watched her leave and then confronted Summer, who was looking down at him with her hands planted in tight fists on her hips. At that moment she was a strict school mistress who lost control and respect from her pupils.

'Did you really have to blast her like that?' Bruno raged. 'My God, Summer. With everything going on, how could you even suggest I would have time to betray you? You should be happy that we have friends who support us; we need them'.

Summer turned away from him as she could not bear to see the disgust and anger in his eyes. Her shoulders shrugged, and she flung her hands towards her eyes. Her breathing hitched, and she began to cry as quietly as she could.

Bruno's temper subsided as rapidly as it had escalated. He hated to see her so hurt, especially as he had been the cause of it. He got up and went to her. Placing his arms around her, he hugged her from behind.

Summer swiftly twirled around and clung tightly to him. This dramatic display of emotion, although clumsy, caused Bruno to return the desperate hold. Just as quickly, Summer moved away from Bruno and smiled up at him. The tears still shimmered in her eyes. 'You're right. I'm sorry. It's just that I love you'.

This sudden admission of feelings was abrupt and inappropriate at this time, leaving Bruno unable to give any kind of reply.

'Well say something'. She giggled, taking his silence to mean shyness. Without waiting for an answer, she took hold of his hand and led him to the dining hall for lunch.

This time Bruno failed to hear the alarm signalling that it was time for a break.

CHAPTER 21

FAREWELL, MY FRIENDS

THE FOUR FRIENDS sat at the table, enthusiastically consuming the exquisite delights arranged before them. It never ceased to amaze Bruno how famished he seemed to be once he smelt and saw the food. No one spoke as they all concentrated on their meal. Even though Summer and Elzbieta refused to mention what had happened previously, Bruno could sense the tension between them. Carlos was oblivious to everything and joyfully tucked into a plate of steaming pasta smothered in a gooey cheese sauce.

Granddad was, once again, on the far side of the room and appeared to be in the middle of some heated debate with his friends. Bruno smiled, taking pleasure from seeing the old man so content. He wondered how much Granddad knew about Harry's plan and what he thought about his involvement in it. It became so important to Bruno to have Granddad's opinion on things that he treasured each word that escaped his wrinkled lips.

Carlos broke Bruno's thoughts. 'What have we got planned for this afternoon?'

'Intense training again'. Bruno grinned when he saw Elzbieta's distressed expression. 'No blood this time, just strategic moves. Formations and battle plans, that kind of thing'.

'You have everything planned? Quite the field marshal, aren't we?' Carlos quipped.

Bruno ignored this. 'I would like all of you to come with me to the amphitheatre straight after we have eaten. You need to see the plans before we tell our soldiers'.

'Yes, sir'. Summer saluted in an attempt at humour. She clearly admired his courage as she looked at him in adoration.

The four laughed together, sweeping away the mood that had previously settled. The conversation lightened and flowed more smoothly. Bruno was pleased to see them all getting on well together again.

Just as he was feeling that things could not get any better, Granddad caught his eye and waved jovially at him. His smile could not have been wider or more loving than it was at that moment, and Bruno felt all his love for the old man stretch towards him in the hope of wrapping itself around, engulfing him with the protection and care that Bruno vowed to give.

Suddenly the ground began to shake. Glasses vibrated across the tables, plates clattered, and cutlery chattered. Ornamental vases toppled and smashed on the floor. A low rumbling warned of the storm that was to follow. Louder and more fiercely the turbulence rattled every bone in every body, causing each stomach to flip uneasily.

At first everyone was silent, listening to the threatening noise and looking feverishly around in an attempt to make sense of what was going on. A chandelier high above them rang like small bells, creating a chaotic melody that grew in intensity before tumbling down and crashing to the ground. Bits of sharp crystal sprang into the air and scattered carelessly over a large circumference, slicing into cheeks and digging into legs and arms.

In panic, both humans and aliens raced around without definite direction; ear-splitting screams and shouts echoed in sharp contrast to the base drone.

Bruno looked for Granddad and saw him advance towards him. He charged like a bull, strong and determined, pushing aside tables and flinging chairs as he went; easily tackling any obstacle in his way. With such speed and agility it was only a matter of seconds before he reached Bruno. Grabbing him by the arm he yelled, 'The pit; we must head for the pit!'

Bruno did not have a clue what the old man was talking about but obeyed and let him lead. Over his shoulder he cried out to the other three, who stared at him blankly, 'Follow me!'

All three joined the sprint until they collided into a current of bodies that swept them up, pulling them along in the same direction. It seemed everyone had the same idea.

They were carried along for some time until they saw a gigantic metal wall. The flow towards it slowed to a trickle and then stopped. Those closest waited. Behind them they heard gunshots and blasts; flickering light blazed and then died, creating a strobe effect. Screams of terror and pain seeped through the explosions as many had not made it to this section of the building.

Without warning, another metal wall shot down from the ceiling, forming a barrier between those inside the room from the devastation beyond.

Bruno looked at Granddad with such sadness that the old man pulled him nearer to comfort him. *How many didn't survive?* tormented Bruno's mind.

The wall in front of them slid up, revealing a steep staircase leading down into the darkness.

'That's the way to the pit. Once we get there, we'll be safe', Granddad whispered in Bruno's ear. He patted him gently on the back. All his energy and strength had disappeared, and the pain that replaced it was back with a vengeance, but Granddad could put up with it. They were safe; Bruno was safe. Slowly the line moved forward as the survivors began to descend. Summer, Elzbieta, and Carlos were ahead of them. The tight collection of bodies dispersed in order to give others space. A massive boom from a room above deafened everyone and arms were instinctively flung out to the side in order to maintain balance. Debris fell like snow, and with it came another boom that cracked the weakened ceiling.

Granddad looked up. Just over where Bruno was standing the fissures gaped open, forming an open mouth ready to throw up the bricks and metal that once were the structure of the building.

It groaned loudly, and without thinking, Granddad darted towards Bruno. Determination was the machine that gunned his movement. Bruno finally saw the ceiling cave in above him and then felt a force push him aside. He collapsed on the floor. Small bits of plaster and dust dropped onto his head.

He turned to where he had been standing, and underneath a thick covering of rubble was a body. As the dust began to settle, the feet and one arm were visible. The shoes, the watch, and the wedding ring looked too familiar … feeling light-headed, Bruno trembled.

'Granddad, no'. His voice cracked. Scrambling towards the heap he began to claw at rocks, throwing them aside as tears fell like a shower down his face. Painful cries became hideous wails. *'No, Granddad!'*

Everything stopped. Even the bombs ceased fire. Everyone stood still and looked fixedly at the boy who cradled the man he cherished. Each one of them said a private prayer of thanks that it was not them in his place. Time seemed to pause in respect for the valiant, great man that now found peace in heaven.

Summer knelt by Bruno's side and placed her hand carefully on his shoulder. 'Come on, Bruno', she soothed, 'we have to go'.

At first Bruno ignored her words, but with mild insistence he complied. Once more he looked at the old man's face and bent forward to kiss his soft cheek. He could still smell the aftershave that Granddad had always insisted on wearing and the shampoo that kept his hair fresh all day long. 'I'll always make you proud of me', he promised.

Summer helped him to his feet, and slowly they headed to the foot of the stairs.

CHAPTER 22

THE VOYAGE INTO SPACE

AFTER DESCENDING THE many flights of stairs, they finally arrived at the pit. Even though the room was lit by an array of lights, it was still quite dark. The room was large and smelt of diesel, metal, and rubber, and aliens were frantically moving around, busily working. The room was actually a cave which appeared to have been hollowed out by force rather than as nature had intended. The scooped-out sides of the walls created patterns that felt smooth to the touch in places and angled to sharp points in others. The stone itself twinkled in the lights, and were a mixture of different particles. The room was cool and devoid of any breeze.

In the centre of the room was a magnificent aircraft unlike anything Bruno had ever seen. It had the familiarity of a space shuttle but also of a cruise ship that had been tipped on its side. There were many round portholes that looked like eyes staring at the people below. The surface of the craft was a dark shade of metallic silver that had been polished to perfection. It truly was a wonder to behold, a trophy of workmanship presented with pride for viewing pleasure.

Bruno froze in amazement and wondered if Granddad had had the chance to see this room or spaceship. Every time he thought about the old man, the pain of his loss clenched his stomach. But all he could think of was Granddad.

Harry emerged from the shadows and took centre stage in front of the craft. For a moment he merely gazed at the people before him, surveying those that survived and counting how many had been lost.

Finally he spoke. 'The day we all feared has come. The Gwarks have attacked us and destroyed our underground home. We are safe here for now, but not for long. We have no choice but to board our ship and go back to Nimara. There we will continue the fight until our fate has been met. Humans, you have the choice of joining us on our mission or going back to your homes. We created a tunnel that will transport you to safe ground far away from here. The Gwarks will not bother with you; their fight is with us. If you wish to leave, then please step over there, and Norman will see you home'.

Everyone turned to where Harry had been pointing, and Bruno was amused to see that Norman was the scientist he had met earlier that day. *Normal Norman,* he thought and managed a weak smile.

At first no one moved, and then a tall, middle-aged man shuffled towards Norman. As if giving others the courage to make a decision, a crowd moved, and one by one joined the increasing group at the other side. No one spoke. No one needed to. After a few moments, Bruno noticed that the only humans to remain were the four of them. Summer, Elzbieta, and Carlos circled Bruno, showing that they would always stand together.

Bruno felt a tug on his shirt and realised Charlie was trying to get his attention. He smiled up at Bruno when a moment later Tim was by Charlie's side. They both were now part of the team.

Harry acknowledged the people that were ready to leave. He smiled affectionately and nodded. 'My deepest gratitude to you all for everything you have done for us. I wish you all a happy life and good health. When you return to your loved ones, they will remember you, as our spell will be lifted'.

'Did you hear that?' Summer whispered excitedly. Bruno had indeed heard the promise Harry made and hoped that one day, he too would be able to return home.

Once the group left with Norman, Harry looked at the four remaining humans and nodded with approval. He was pleased to see they had stayed, although he never considered them making any other choice.

The ground began to tremble, and for a moment all four of them panicked, thinking the Gwarks had already burst their way into the pit. Steam gushed out of the base of the spacecraft, hissing as it belched out its fumes. White clouds formed as the steam hit the cool air and swirled hypnotically before them. Lights flicked on inside the craft, shining out like torches from every porthole. The giant had come to life, ready to make its long voyage into space.

Fear and excitement mixed as one by one people boarded the craft. As soon as everyone was onboard, the spacecraft shot upwards as smoothly and noiselessly as silk moved by a gentle breeze. Like a knife through soft butter, it cut through the ground and burst into the open air. Before anyone could witness this incredible sight it had disappeared, heading up beyond the sky.

CHAPTER 23

INSIDE THE SPACESHIP

BRUNO HAD TIGHTLY shut his eyes, waiting for the lift-off. His heart thumped and his legs felt weak. Pins and needles pricked his feet as they performed gymnastics over his skin. His breathing began to quicken, so he focused all his attention on steadying it. He could imagine the movement of his heart and felt the pumping of his pulse in his arms and head. Creating a steady rhythm of inhaling deeply and exhaling slowly, his whole body finally relaxed. Everything around him was silent. In this state of concentration, he blocked everyone else out, leaving him in the silence of his own bubble, floating away with his thoughts.

Summer sat next to him. Her expression was tense, as was her posture. Her muscles ached with the tension forced upon them. Her clawed hands, vice-like in Bruno's, had turned white. Negative thoughts raced around in her head like trapped mice, and she was unable to hold on to any one of them at any given time. 'What if I can't breathe? What if I explode? What if … what if …?'

Elzbieta was in the seat next to her and then Carlos. Both looked strangely at peace; vague smiles surfaced, showing that the fire of excitement had been ignited within them. The only visible sign of anxiety was in the fact that they too held hands tightly, enough to cause them to quiver.

They could hear the build-up of the engine as it whistled a single note that gradually and smoothly increased in volume and changed to two octaves higher. Without warning, each body thrust back, sucked into the seats that held them. Each head was forced into the soft pillow behind that protected them from the impact.

The sensation was strange but not unpleasant. After a few moments of feeling weighed down, there was a pop in both ears that was as light as a tinkle of a bell and as gentle as a bubble imploding. All sense of stress released, flowing out of the fingertips and toes, leaving the person feeling almost euphoric. All noise was annihilated, and the silence that followed was tranquil, adding to the peaceful atmosphere.

After a few minutes, a bell pinged, and all the aliens clicked open their seatbelts and started to move towards the door. The four humans looked at them, bewildered.

'I thought we just stay in these seats', Summer said to the rest of the group.

'What, for three days?' Charlie popped up seemingly from nowhere. 'I want to show you the rest of the ship. Also, I need to escort you to your rooms. What would you like to do first? Would you prefer to see your rooms or a guided tour?' Smiling enthusiastically, he jumped up and down, making his head bop involuntarily.

All eyes looked towards Bruno. He was still in command, even to his friends. 'Tour I guess'. He decided, but looked at the others to see if they approved.

The small group headed towards the door with Charlie in the lead. From time to time he turned around and grinned up at them; it was obvious that he enjoyed his newfound responsibility.

Once through the door, Bruno noticed they were confronted with a tubular corridor that was covered all the way around with the same metal that adorned the outside. The portholes appeared much larger from the inside, and to Bruno's amazement, all he could see was a black sky with millions of twinkling stars. Mesmerised, he gravitated towards the thick glass and, with his nose touching the coolness, he looked more closely. A star shot across with its tail blazing a blue light. Its path was inches from Bruno's face, and it made him flinch. Stepping closer again, he could see that the sky was not totally black but shades of colour – purple, yellow, and red streaks that formed in places and waved like the sea. It was the most beautiful sight he had ever seen.

He turned back towards the others, who were also looking out the various windows.

Charlie stood waiting patiently in the centre of the corridor. 'If you think this is spectacular, just wait until you get to Nimara'. Charlie smiled proudly. 'You must meet my family when we get there'. His face lit up.

'Your family?' Carlos enquired. None of them thought about Charlie having a family of his own as he looked and acted as though he still clung to his mother's apron strings.

'Yes'. He nodded energetically. 'My wife and three children – two boys and a baby girl'.

'It would be lovely to meet them'. Elzbieta responded with equal fervour.

Charlie beamed with such zeal that his cheeks flushed and he began to skip on the spot. Briskly he turned and advanced through the corridor. The others followed, eager to see as much of the ship as possible.

There were so many rooms, and each one was spacious and luxurious. Bruno kept forgetting that he was in a spaceship on a mission, as everything around him catered for leisure and relaxation. There were three different eating areas that offered a huge variety of meals; two swimming pools, a sauna, a music room with so many different instruments; a library with a wealth of books; and rooms where people could just meet and enjoy the company of others. Every room was elaborately decorated with flamboyant designs that still managed to remain tasteful.

Throughout the guided tour, Charlie babbled on, heartily pointing this way and that in an attempt to show his companions every little detail of the ship.

'We are just travelling for three days, aren't we?' Summer was suddenly anxious.

'Yes, but imagine what a great three days it will be', Carlos answered, still in awe of the sights he was taking in.

'I'll show you your rooms, but first we need to see the games room'. Charlie remained professional and serious about keeping to his planned route.

At this Carlos perked up, sharply raising his head and straightening his back in a way that reminded Bruno of a meerkat sensing something of interest. 'A games room?'

Charlie nodded. 'Yes. We have all the latest consoles and other gadgets that you enjoy on earth. To be honest, I rather like them too'.

'Oh, I don't think we'll see Carlos for the rest of the journey now'. Elzbieta laughed.

It took some persistence to drag Carlos out of the games room. Once inside, he was hooked and wanted to try everything. The others, however, were curious about their rooms.

Each of them was allocated his and her own room, which consisted of a double bed, cupboards full of garments to wear, and a bathroom.

Summer was excited to see that the clothes were not the same cream-coloured uniform they all wore underground but a variety of colours and styles. There was even makeup and jewellery in one of the drawers.

Bruno could not wait to try out the double bed. Elzbieta was enthralled with the bath. It was so large and deep, with steps leading down to it. An array of bath products was neatly shelved, and straight away she sniffed at each bottle. 'I'm in heaven!' she exclaimed.

'Well, here's to a week in space'. Carlos cheered happily.

Chapter 24

THE BATTLE PLANS

BRUNO WAS WALKING through a field covered with wildflowers and thick-stemmed deep green grass that tickled his legs. He smelled the fresh and sweet fragrance of the foliage and felt the gentle warm breeze that combed through his hair. The sun was bright and emanated a welcomed glow, and the sky was a clear blue. Birds flew lazily and chirped to one another.

'I knew you would visit me'. Granddad was walking by his side and smiled with adoration at Bruno.

'How could I not visit you? I miss you so much', Bruno replied warmly. He noticed the old man did not seem so old anymore. His eyes shined as brightly as the sun, and his cheeks were pink with health. His hair remained as white as snow but seemed thicker and shinier. He walked briskly with not a single trace of pain in his step.

'So, leading an army are you, my boy?' Granddad's tone was clipped with pride.

'Yes. I have to'.

'Don't you mean you want to?' Granddad teased as he always did.

Bruno smiled and without thinking cuddled the old man tightly. He buried his face in the gentle man's chest and felt his warm arms envelop him. Bruno clung on and did not want to let go.

As he woke, he heard the words Granddad whispered: 'I love you, dear boy, and I'm so proud of you'.

Bruno sat up in his bed and wept.

After some time he managed to breathe steadily and dried his eyes. He walked to the bathroom with the feeling of misery and heartache that knotted his insides. He hoped he would have such dreams again.

Once he was ready, he opened the door and was faced with Charlie grinning up at him. Seeing Bruno's eyes were red and puffed, he stopped grinning and replaced the look with concern. He remained silent for a few seconds, thinking of what to say.

He decided not to draw attention to the obvious fact that Bruno was upset and just relayed the message he was sent to give. 'Harry would like you to see him now. I will escort you to his office'. In his usual manner, he turned swiftly and began to move down the corridor.

Sighing, Bruno followed. He did not have the energy and lacked curiosity to ask why he was needed.

Once they arrived outside Harry's office, Charlie paused. He quickly hugged him, gave a sympathetic smile, and left. Surprised by this, Bruno shook his head and entered the room.

This office was exactly like the one in the underground, which told Bruno that Harry did not like change. *Well, if something works …* he thought, and managed a wistful smile.

Harry got straight to the point. 'Bruno, we need to discuss your procedure once we land in Nimara. We've been alerted to the fact that currently there are a thousand Gwarks advancing to our capital city. They have destroyed every town and village in their path and killed many'. He bent his head in anguish. 'They are working at a very fast pace, and so far no one has managed to even slow them down. You must have plans in place. I will show you a map of the city and where the Gwarks are at the moment. We must ensure that we use each of our soldiers' strengths to the maximum and organise our advance carefully. You have fewer than three days now to perfect your ideas, and I will keep you updated on what is happening in Nimara. Your first step is to list the strengths of each of our men and women and decide what part they will play in battle'.

'You want this information by tomorrow?' Bruno asked.

'I know there is not much time, as time is not on our side. As soon as we land, we must be ready to fight'.

The idea of using all of the wonderful facilities on the ship suddenly faded away. It was work as usual. Bruno had to tell the others, who would not be impressed with the tasks he was to assign them. He was ashamed of these thoughts. They had made their decision in the pit. They had chosen to help the aliens, and a promise had been given. They knew it was dangerous and hard work, but it was the path of their choosing.

Bruno turned towards Harry once more and firmly announced, 'You'll have the information by tomorrow morning'. With this he strode determinedly out of the room.

After gaining the register and photographs of those aboard the ship, he informed the others to meet him in his room as soon as they could. As he waited, he began to look through the list of names and photographs. This was not going to be an easy task.

One by one they entered his room, and to his amazement took the assignment in their stride. They discussed each person on the register, sometimes agreeing quickly and at others arguing passionately. Those that they were more familiar with were easy to decide, and notes were added to their names. However, there remained a list of names and faces that needed attention. They decided they would test each of the people on this list in the afternoon and find their strengths and weaknesses.

Bruno delegated. 'Carlos, here is the list that you will be working with. Summer, here are yours, and Elzbieta these are yours. I have my list as well. Good luck. When you've finished, meet me in the diner. We'll share our findings while we eat'.

Each of them went their separate ways without a word. They all knew how important it was to get this right.

CHAPTER 25

THE TEST

Carlos decided to hold his tests in the games room. This idea was justified by the fact that by playing the console games, the person would display his or her dexterity and ability to solve problems. Physical abilities could be tested through the use of a football, by skipping rope, and using other items available in the room. He rearranged the room until he was satisfied and stood back to gloat about what he had done. He was ready, and with clipboard in hand, he called in his first 'victim'.

Firstly he made the alien play a game where he had to drive a racing car at full throttle. Carlos cheered and jumped excitedly while the alien wobbled with the motion of the turns he made the car take. At times he whimpered quietly as his eyes were strained on the car's progress. When he crashed he jerked, letting go of the controller, and rubbed his arms trying to massage his aching muscles. He then was made to play several problem-solving games. After that he had to skip for ten minutes and then use the punching bag. Carlos realised the only findings he had was that the alien was relatively strong and extremely fit. He needed something more than this.

'You want to know what my skill is?' the alien asked.

Carlos looked at him and shrugged. 'Tell me'.

The alien rubbed his hands together and a ball of fire emerged. He held them out to allow the fire to flicker steadily. They did not seem to burn him even though Carlos could feel the heat from where he was standing.

'I am forbidden to do it here, but if I throw them, they explode anything they land on. They are like your bombs. I prefer to use them to warm up a cold place or boil water'.

Mouth agape, Carlos stared at the globes of fire. 'I think that's all I need to know. Send the next one in please'.

Summer had decided to use one of the swimming pools to test her aliens. She had planned to make each one swim as many lengths as possible and see how long they could hold their breath underwater. After this, she wanted them to carry heavy objects from one side of the pool to the other.

When the first alien came into the room, Summer did not get the opportunity to give the first command. The girl slid into the pool and manipulated the water as though it was a solid object. She created a whirlpool and made it spin above her head. Not a single droplet was left in the pool. As the whirlpool spun it changed shape, becoming a gigantic sharp spear.

'If I want, I can throw this and it will solidify into ice and split anything in its path. Of course I do not use it for that purpose. I prefer to let children ride in the water just like the roundabouts in your recreational fields'.

Elzbieta did not have any plans in place as she decided to take the direct approach. She held her interviews in the library and asked each alien to show her what he or she could do. The results were quick and the job was done efficiently. She was impressed to see how many different skills the aliens possessed. Some could make people do whatever they commanded whilst others could turn into smoke or become part of an object to camouflage themselves. What she found interesting was that none of the aliens realised how useful their given talent would be in battle. Violence did not enter their minds at all, even though they knew how dangerous their abilities could be.

They all met in the diner and were eager to share their findings. With such abilities, there was a chance of winning the fight against the Gwarks; they just needed to be shown how to use them effectively.

Bruno summed up. 'They are fast and can teleport; they never tire and have amazing talents. We just need to decide how we can use them in battle, give everyone responsibilities'.

Happy with the way the day went, the friends tucked into a delicious meal of burgers, chips, and Coke. They felt they deserved a treat.

Later that evening, Bruno returned to his room with the list of names, photographs, and the information asked for by Harry. He placed the papers on the desk and glanced at them. They'd worked so hard today, and their efforts were productive. Bruno had begun to form battle plans with every soldier assigned to a task. All he had left was to decide what his three friends would do. This would be the toughest decisions of all. He would be responsible for the lives of his devoted friends. Would he be sending them into victory or to certain death?

CHAPTER 26

THIS IS NIMARA

THE THREE DAYS passed quickly, and all too soon Bruno was counting down the hours before they would land in Nimara. Most of his time and energy had been spent preparing his troops for battle. At first the aliens were horrified to learn they must use their abilities violently, but they understood they needed to defend their planet and their loved ones.

Reluctantly, he had decided that Summer, Elzbieta, and Carlos should lead the army into battle with him, standing side by side. They worked best as a team, so it was with no surprise that they had expected this.

Charlie was becoming more and more excited about being reunited with his family and grinned crazily, wide-eyed, frantically flapping his hands. 'Only two hours to go', he declared loudly.

Bruno did not share Charlie's enthusiasm as he feared the landing as much as he had the lift-off.

Soon an alarm signalled all passengers to return to the main seating area where they had to be securely buckled in. The four of them returned to the same seats and waited in silence. Each was deep in thought. They all tried to ignore the fact that they were fast approaching the moment when they would have to step into battle.

Bruno realised this section was deprived of windows, so they would not be able to even catch a glimpse of the planet until they took their first steps on it.

Summer clutched Bruno's hand and winked at him. Bruno responded by blowing her a kiss, which made her beam and wriggle her fingers between his so that her hold was even firmer.

The engine began to whistle in a similar way to the take-off, and Bruno closed his eyes once more. The ship slowly descended, and this time Bruno felt as though he was floating on a fluffy cloud, gently gliding towards his destination. Even when landing, there was not a single bump. The ship merely ceased to move. The bell pinged once more, and Bruno braced himself for his first sight of Nimara.

The door slid open with a whispered sigh, and one by one the aliens stepped out into the fresh air. Bruno was anxious but could not wait to experience the view of another planet. As he got closer to the front of the line, he felt a warm breeze sweep into the ship and a glowing light throwing its beams at the floor. As he approached the doorway he shielded his eyes; the light was intense. Once fully adjusted to the sudden brightness, he looked around slowly, trying to take in everything at once. It was truly beautiful.

The sky was velvet blue tinted with ribbons of deep red that waved like silk cloth, flapping in the cool air. Stars shined vibrantly and twinkled, reminding him of randomly scattered glitter. Just like in his dream, he saw two suns and three moons harmoniously sharing the sky. The trees formed lines across the field as if standing at attention, respectfully greeting the passengers. Majestic buildings proudly sat on ground covered with thick green grass and exotic flowers that curtseyed, bowing their heads with the weight of the multicoloured petals. The buildings were of a variety of shapes and sizes, built out of materials that shined, reflecting the light of the stars. Lining the sides of the path leading to one of the largest buildings were countless aliens who skipped happily and cheered loudly.

As the aliens from the ship set foot on the ground, they caught sight of their loved ones and ran towards them, colliding, hugging, kissing, and shedding tears of joy.

Bruno caught sight of Charlie, who was running this way and that, eyeing each face in the crowd, searching for his family. His head bopped up and down as he jumped to see farther into the depth of the crowd but was so far unsuccessful.

As Bruno stepped down towards the ground, Summer was by his side. She gasped and cried out, 'So beautiful!' It was at this point that Bruno became aware that they could breathe naturally. They did not wear space helmets like in the movies back home. However, he did not think this as being strange at all as the aliens breathed Earth's air without any problem.

Elzbieta and Carlos were behind, and they too were captivated by the scene in front of them. Together they walked towards the magnificent building, following the others.

Bruno continued to watch Charlie and started to get a bad feeling about what he was seeing. Many aliens had already died at the hands of the Gwarks, but Bruno chose to remain silent. Voicing his concerns could tempt fate.

They all advanced towards the mighty building, whose entrance gaped like a giant mouth yawning widely. As each alien stepped through the threshold, they disappeared into the throat and were swallowed up into the darkness that lay beyond. Bruno eagerly quickened his pace, leading Summer by the hand, almost pulling her along.

'Hey, what's the hurry?' Summer asked in mock humour. Her eyes were everywhere and did not settle for long in any given direction. The new sights were overwhelming, and she needed time to capture each aspect of them.

Without answering, Bruno strode through the colossal door into a vast hallway that appeared to go on forever. Both sides of the hall were adorned with sconces that burned fiercely, lighting the way forward. The floor, walls, and ceiling were made of marble in which intricate carvings created pictures of all sorts. History was eternally etched for future commemoration. The overall effect was stupendous.

The hallway eventually opened up into an immense room where all the aliens from the ship congregated. Some still clung to their loved ones, whilst others were engulfed in deep conversations. Harry stood in the centre, watching and waiting patiently.

At the sides of the room, aliens dressed in uniform stood erect, ready for their next command. Preparations were underway for battle here as well.

Charlie flew across the room like a comet, questioning every alien that he bumped into. His face was now a bluish white and his cheeks flushed alarmingly. His movements were erratic as he flickered to and fro, using his ability to move from one place to another too quickly for the eye to see. A taller alien, who had the air of authority, brought Charlie to an abrupt stop as he clamped his large hand on his shoulder. Charlie looked up at the other alien with reverence and stared at him wide eyed, searching for answers. The larger alien made him sit down and spoke gently. Charlie listened intently to every word and with each moment his excitement, fears, panic, and hopes withered and died. He sagged as though everything drained from him and left just an empty shell.

Bruno watched all of this and without conscious thought stepped towards him. Feeling nauseated, he shortened the distance between them until he stood before the broken being.

Charlie slowly raised his large head and gazed upon his friend. There was no adoration in his eyes or even a flicker of emotion. Glazed like a child's doll, his eyes were unmoving.

Bruno's heart wept for Charlie, the sweet alien, as he knew he had lost his wife and children, whom he loved more than anything in the whole universe. They were his reason for living; without them, he was nothing.

Bruno knelt and could not find the words to console him. Instead he held him tightly in his arms. After a few moments, the once-lively, fun-loving alien howled with such pain that his whole body shook.

Bruno just held him tighter.

After some time, Charlie managed to tell Bruno what he had been told. The events leading to his family's death was more tragic than Bruno could have ever imagined.

Knowing Charlie was soon to return, his wife had the idea of preparing a huge welcome home for him. She was determined to buy the best ingredients for his first meal back home and to surprise him with expensive gifts. They had often visited a town some distance to the south of the city, and on countless occasions Charlie had made his usual return to a particular shop that sold unusual pets. He had found a particularly rare dragon that had been carefully incubated for two years before it finally hatched. Its wings were every shade of the rainbow and glistened like silk as it swished them up and down. Its beak shined like gold, and the two beady eyes were as black as the night sky. It sung like a siren and could enchant the most unfeeling beast alive. Charlie wanted it, and his wife was made fully aware of this. Both knew it was far too expensive, and with little ones to look after, it became a mere dream. It did not stop Charlie from constantly visiting the shop to at least get a glimpse of the unique pet. Unknown to him, his wife had saved money carefully and finally had enough to buy and maintain the dragon.

Just two days earlier, she had set off with the children in order to buy the dream pet and other items for her husband's return. She had been totally unaware of how far the Gwarks had advanced. As they pushed their way through the town, Charlie's wife and children became one of the many families who suffered at the hands of the enemy. All because she loved her husband and wanted to give him a welcome home he would never forget.

Chapter 27

INTO BATTLE

Leaving Charlie in his time of need was difficult for Bruno, and he felt as though he was letting him down. However, Charlie needed the time to mourn in his own way.

Harry called to Bruno and gestured to the other three humans to come to him. When all were together, Harry apologised.

'I know you have just landed, but time is not on our side. The Gwarks are at this moment surrounding this city. They are preparing to strike any time now'. His voice had taken on a sense of urgency that for once left his true feelings of fear and despair naked for all to see.

This vulnerability frightened Bruno, as he had grown accustomed to the leading alien being composed and instilling in others a sense of calm and confidence. Had the situation become so desperate that even this dignified and strong alien had become a quivering wreck?

As though sensing his thoughts, Harry slowed his pace. 'We have an extra five hundred soldiers who have been trained as well. They have followed your strict training regime too, Bruno. I have been monitoring your progress at all stages and relayed your techniques to my people here. Each soldier's talent is known and recorded alongside your list. I am afraid it is now or never. We must send you out to fight now'.

Bruno froze and moved his mouth, trying to voice his thoughts. Seeing his moment of panic, Elzbieta took control. 'So where do we collect our armour and weapons?'

Harry regarded Elzbieta with relief. 'Behind me is a room with all of your needs catered to. Choose what you want, and make ready your army. In exactly one hour you will leave this building and go out into the fields. You do not need to cover every side of the city. Whilst we were experimenting underground on Earth, the people here have been doing the same. They have created a shield that will protect the city from practically every side. However, there is a weakness; the shield is made of a solid substance but in order to include a doorway outside, one part of it had to be thinned down. If the Gwarks were to attack from that side the shield would collapse and we would become completely defenceless. The doorway is necessary as we do not just want to protect this city, many lives are at stake. Too many have been lost already'.

'Don't we know it?' All eyes turned to Charlie, who had silently joined them. 'Let's go get them. They took my life already. I have nothing left to live for. I want them to feel pain like I do'. He cast his eyes downwards, and Bruno could see how circumstance had changed the little alien. His innocence and hunger for experience had been stripped away, leaving a hard, bitter soul who needed revenge. Time helps heal the wounds of sorrow but can never fully get rid of the scars. It was with great pity that Bruno realised the Charlie of old no longer existed.

Harry averted his thoughts. 'Bruno, remember the pill. You'll know when to take it. Just use your gut feelings'. He opened his hand to reveal a small golden box. Bruno took the box, placed it safely in his shirt pocket, and nodded to Harry to show he understood.

Bruno led the way to the next room. Dutifully, the soldiers from the ship followed. Bruno was once more amazed by how meticulous the aliens were. On one side of the room the outfits were arranged in size order. The outer layer of the suit was like a hard shell, and when he knocked on it with his knuckles, it made a heavy clunking sound. Picking it up, he was astounded by the lack of weight. Even though it looked heavy, it was as light as a feather. On the other side of the room, the weapons hung in rows, ready for the choosing. Some of them he had seen before underground and understood their usage. However, there were others that he had not become familiarised with and so decided to stay away from them.

Bruno chose two guns and a belt decorated with pellets. The belt was similar to a bullet belt, but these pellets were far more destructive. Just by throwing them, they would sail through the air at great distances and obliterate anything in their path.

On a table in the centre of the room were packages of food and drink. They were not prepared for pleasure but for survival. Bruno took some of the packages, and once fully armoured and ready for battle, he watched the others. There was a tense atmosphere and a real sense of urgency; everyone knew what they were about to commit themselves to.

Charlie argued with Tim, who was trying to pick a suit for himself.

'I'm not letting you come. Your parents need you here, you idiot. I'm not letting you go out there!' Charlie roared.

'It's my choice; I need to be part of this!' Tim shouted back.

Bruno reluctantly stepped in. 'We need as many men as we can. Tim, get yourself ready; we're about to go'.

Both aliens stopped bickering. Charlie regarded Tim sadly and then shot Bruno a piercing glare. Bruno felt he deserved this as yet again he was leading such wonderful beings to certain death. Tim was not strong but he was determined, and Bruno hoped this would be enough to see him through.

Once every soldier was ready, they moved in single file towards the back of the building. Their exit would be through a narrow door that, once opened, would reveal it to be a foot thick and made of the same metal as the spaceship. A siren would signal when the soldiers would be allowed to advance into the open air, as the protective shield that surrounded the city would be temporarily lifted. Adequate time would be given for them to leave the city as long as they were efficient and kept to a rapid pace. A siren would be sounded once more to notify everyone that the shield was on again.

They did not wait more than a few moments before the siren bellowed, and the door automatically moved to reveal the night sky. Wind blasted their faces, as if warning them of their impending doom. With Bruno in the lead, they marched forward. A winding path guided them to a humongous gate that settled snugly between the vast metal walls that protected the city. These gates again opened them. Once on the other side, Bruno stopped and waited for everyone to pass through the gate.

Charlie had taken up the rear of the line with Tim in front of him. From time to time his friend turned around and gave a weak smile that failed to reach his eyes. He was shivering with fright but did not break the rhythm that his quivering feet made on the soil. Charlie merely watched him, showing neither concern nor sympathy. His face was set and unreadable.

Once everyone was almost through, the siren sounded once more. This time the tone was one of panic as it shrieked its caution. Charlie and Tim had reached the border of the city; one step was all they needed to take and there would be no turning back.

Charlie slammed his hand down firmly on his friend's shoulder and spun him around. 'Forgive me', he said gently; his voice was deep and smooth and soft as velvet, hardly audible above the cacophony. 'I cannot let you do this'.

With all his strength he shoved Tim back, away from the gate. Tim lost his footing and fell crashing down on his back. He gawped at Charlie in astonishment. Charlie smiled down at his faithful friend and swiftly ran through the gate. Before Tim could get to his feet, the shield clamped down, making a secure barrier between them.

On the other side, Charlie lingered in the direction of where Tim had stood just seconds before. He bowed his head, raised his hand slowly, and touched the barricade lightly with his fingertips.

'Be safe, my friend', he mouthed.

The soldiers had witnessed this and said nothing. There was nothing to say.

Chapter 28

FACING THE GWARKS

The thunder of feet stomping on the ground was heard, and occasional cheers and shrieks echoed from across the field. The Gwarks were not very far from the city limits, and they were quickly approaching.

Bruno raised his hand to get everyone's attention. 'Get into position!' He shouted forcefully, hoping to hide the fear that welled inside him. As soon as he said those words, there was a rush of bodies darting to and fro. Those with the ability to bulldoze the heavyset Gwarks were at the front; the rest of the soldiers were behind. Each one was fully aware of his or her responsibility during battle. Some had to create as much damage as possible while others would defend the troops.

On the horizon, a mass of dots emerged, and very quickly these dots became lumps which formed into bodies of the beasts. With every heartbeat they closed in on the trembling soldiers. Against the riot of noise made by the opposition, the silence of the soldiers was eerie. All waited for Bruno to signal their next move.

Bruno stood still, watching the advancing enemy. Just as he had dreamt, the Gwarks were tall and heavily built masses of muscle which ran with athletic dexterity. Each carried a different weapon, all of which looked extremely violent and able to kill with ease. Their faces were hog-like and were fixed with determination and hatred.

It was at this point that it became crystal clear that fighting against the Gwarks was complete madness.

Although he would have preferred to give up, he raised his arm and bellowed with all his might, 'Charge!'

All the soldiers stormed towards the enemy with Bruno, Summer, Elzbieta, and Carlos in the lead. The battle had commenced; there was no turning back.

The two sides collided, but remarkably the soldiers were able to use their abilities to wound the first row of Gwarks. Some tumbled down in agony, creating a carpet of flesh that became instantly crushed by stomping feet. Blood poured from various orifices, splashing like paint on the soldiers that remained standing. Guns fired like lasers, the stench of burning meat was overwhelming as soldiers from both sides became part of the barbeque.

Bruno was amazed at how well his soldiers were bearing up, and the hope of winning did not seem like a ludicrous notion anymore. Each person fought bravely, putting heart and soul into succeeding against the Gwarks. Fire flew like comets and burst explosively into the enemy. Some of the aliens used the wind to push back the Gwarks and cause the dust to flick up and blind them. Where possible, others created shields so the brutal attacks made on weaker aliens were futile.

Elzbieta, raging like a bull, was barraging two Gwarks with powerful punches and swinging her sword, which sliced into them. Although determined, it was obvious she was tiring. Carlos, who had noticed that her courageous efforts would not hold them off for long, ran directly towards her. Without thinking, he plunged between her and the attacking Gwarks, instantly creating a barrier that kept Elzbieta safe. Before he had time to do anything else, a gun was fired into his chest. The laser created a hole the size of a tennis ball, and a black ring fizzed with the intense heat as the edges were cauterised.

Carlos gaped, a look of confusion on his face, and then fell to the ground. Elzbieta collapsed to her knees beside him. The two Gwarks were already engaged in a fight against three aliens, but she was no longer concerned with them. She grasped hold of Carlos and held his head up. His breathing became shallow and rattled with the blood that bubbled in his throat. A stream of the blood trickled out of the corner of his mouth.

Elzbieta looked down at her faithful friend and pleaded, 'Carlos, stay with me. Hang on, and I'll get you out of this. You'll be okay'.

Carlos stared up at the girl he loved, and with a weak and heavy hand, he placed his fingers gently against her cheek. She took hold of that hand and kissed it before returning it to her cheek. The blood sprayed out of his mouth each time he choked, and the rattle became a gurgle. Carlos managed to smile at Elzbieta adoringly, and then the light in his eyes vanished as he died.

Elzbieta wept, still holding Carlos in her arms. All around her the battle continued. She whispered in prayer, 'Mother of Christ, I beg you, look after my Carlos'.

She lovingly lowered Carlos back on the ground, and for the last time stroked his hair. She stood up, and with all the pain and sorrow she felt, she screamed. Like a white eagle, strong and proud, she swooped on her enemy. She would avenge Carlos's death.

Bruno caught sight of her and gasped. She looked so strong and beautiful. Graceful yet deadly, she slashed at heads and thrust at stomachs; each Gwark in her path fell.

Switching his focus, Bruno could see the Gwarks had become outnumbered. This was it; they would win this battle. He felt a mixture of relief and pride in his achievements. The Nimarian nation would be saved. His thoughts returned to Carlos, and his heart sank. How could he be dead? Even though he had seen him lying on the ground, it felt more like a horrid nightmare that he would wake up from. Why did there have to be such losses?

Suddenly, one of the Gwarks put a horn to his lips, and an ear-piercing note roared out of it. Bruno felt a sense of dread as he wondered what the purpose of doing this was. It did not take long before his question was answered.

Above the shouts and screams, a low thunderous beat could be heard. The ground beneath their feet vibrated with the heavy stomping feet that raced towards them. More Gwarks were called to join the fight. They would be full of energy and strength, unlike the soldiers here who were exhausted and in many cases wounded.

CHAPTER 29

THE BATTLE CONTINUES

A HERD OF galloping Gwarks burst into view as they charged full throttle towards the battleground. A cloud trailed behind them as they kicked the dust into the air with each step. Their hog-like faces flashed with anger as they snorted streams of mist from their snouts.

Bruno's soldiers turned to face the new approaching rivals, and each of them froze for a moment in sheer terror.

Charlie jumped into the air and turned towards the other aliens. He stayed floating above them. His high-pitched scream hurt Bruno's ears. Charlie's face quickly appeared to melt and then change shape. His teeth became enlarged and pointed, sharp as needles. Although Bruno was more prepared to see their true form, he still shuddered at the sight of the gruesome appearance. Once Charlie's transformation was complete, all the other aliens followed suit. They were not going to give up the fight, and changing into their natural form appeared to gain them renewed strength.

Bruno realised this was the time he was meant to take the pill. He remembered what Harry had told him: 'Use your gut instinct. You will know when the time is right'. Bruno knew the time was in fact not only right but urgent.

He pulled the small box out of his trouser pocket and held it between his finger and thumb. Dropping the gun to free his other hand, he lifted the lid. The pill sat in the centre; it looked so harmless.

Bruno stared at it and froze. What if he changed and never returned to his natural state? How painful would the process of changing be?

Time was not on his side, and the Gwarks had already joined the fight.

But he failed to take the pill.

*

Elzbieta watched and then glanced at Summer, who was also watching Bruno. If he did not take the pill, the battle would be lost. Losing patience, Elzbieta threw down her sword and ran towards Bruno. She snatched the box from his hands, removed the pill, and without hesitation swallowed it.

Agony pulsed through her entire body, and she howled. She shook violently and fell to the floor. Within seconds her body appeared to dissolve as her bones had turned to jelly. Her shape had become completely unrecognisable. Her howls spiralled into a high-pitched scream, similar to the one Charlie had made only a few moments ago. Her flesh became more solid until she became one of the aliens.

Her sharp pointed teeth snapped together as though she was trying to get used to her new form. She stood on unstable feet for a while and then crouched. She looked at Bruno, and then one large eye winked. Pushing off the ground, she rocketed into the sky. With such speed, she dived back down and levelled with the ground.

Maintaining her speed she swooped towards the Gwarks and bolted through them. On impact, each of the Gwarks exploded like bloody fireworks, and body parts scattered across the field. All the aliens cheered excitedly and also took flight. Following Elzbieta's lead, they rammed the enemy. The field had become a slaughterhouse as everything was painted red with blood.

Bruno and Summer were left to observe this gory but magnificent sight. Elzbieta was amazing. With gusto she took on as many Gwarks as she could and moved around with incredible agility. Together the aliens created intricate patterns with their movements, confusing the enemy and taking each one by surprise. In one final flourish of volcanic eruptions of blood and limbs, the battle was finally over.

The aliens gathered together with Bruno and Summer and jumped around, bubbling with excitement, grasping each other tightly and shouting in celebration. Some cried with overflowing emotion.

Charlie stood aside and gave a wistful smile as he surveyed the others. He was happy that his world was saved, but his losses weighed heavily.

Bruno and Summer tried to find Elzbieta amongst the dancing aliens but could not see her straight away. Finally, farther off, Summer spotted her. Elzbieta, still in alien form, knelt facing away from the others. Her face was buried in her hands, and by the way her body shook, it was obvious she was crying.

Summer walked towards her, followed closely by Bruno. Gingerly she touched her shoulder, which caused Elzbieta to flinch. She remained facing the other direction and refused to look at her two friends. She knew she looked unsightly and did not want anyone to see her like this. She hoped she would change back to normal soon and did not care how painful it would be.

Summer understood Elzbieta's need for privacy, and taking Bruno by the hand, walked away. Summer felt complete admiration for Elzbieta as what she did was the ultimate sacrifice for her friends.

Chapter 30

BACK IN THE CITY

ONCE EVERYONE HAD calmed down, it was time to return to the city and give the others the good news. Each soldier marched wearily, trudging slowly with bent backs and wobbly knees. Exhausted and wounded, they began their journey back. Although covered in gore and dust, their smiles were wide. For the first time, a sense of calm had been restored and safety was an old, welcomed friend. To all of them, the air smelled sweeter than ever, the wind's touch softer. The blue sky was bright and clear, and the sun beamed joyously down on them as though in praise of their success. Each soldier saw their world with a new sight. The realisation of what could have been lost was frightening, and they silently promised to not take what they have for granted.

Summer and Bruno walked steadily in front of the tatty line while Elzbieta remained at the back. Bruno occasionally glanced back to check on her. He wanted to console her as well as thank her for what she had done. But she was stubborn, and any attempt to approach her was met with hostility. It was best to leave her alone for now, and let her decide when she wanted comforting. The feeling of being helpless frustrated Bruno, but he had to be patient.

As they reached the city limits, they realised the shield had already been lifted. Bruno still found it difficult to believe how quickly the aliens knew what was going on. He wondered if they were telepathic as well. If so, it would not have surprised him as they were such fascinating beings with abilities beyond the imagination, yet they remained so humble.

They made their way back to the building they had left just a few hours earlier. It seemed like a lifetime ago.

Harry stood at the large door and waited for them to arrive. He was clearly elated.

Inside the building, the other aliens were celebrating the victory as they loudly danced and sang. The word that Nimara was saved was sent to every city, town, and village, and similar displays of joy were displayed all over the planet.

Harry grinned when he saw the troop coming towards him and began to run towards them. Remembering his place as leader, he stopped abruptly and took a deep breath to gain control of his emotions. He began to walk regally and waved.

Bruno and Summer were the first to meet him.

'Even though you are human, you are true to your word. From deep within my heart, I thank you'. Harry bowed to them. He could see two were missing. 'Where are your friends?'

Summer exchanged a sad glance with Bruno, and they both dipped their heads in despair. 'Carlos is no longer with us'. Bruno paused for a moment as his voice broke with sorrow. 'Elzbieta is at the back. She needs to change to her natural form'.

Harry looked surprised. 'The pill?' He looked at Bruno, who had lowered his eyes in shame. 'I'll see to her, as she will need to be cared for until the process is over. Come inside; you need to eat, drink, and have plenty of rest'.

As soon as they all had entered, the aliens inside hollered with excited cheers and expressed their gratefulness with vibrant jubilation. Everyone wanted to shake Bruno's hand and pat him on the back.

Charlie caught up with him and hugged him.

'You were so brave out there, Charlie', Bruno praised him.

Charlie responded by hugging him even harder.

Tim bobbed between the dancing aliens and smiled when he saw Charlie. As soon as he was close to him he shouted, 'Don't ever push me again'.

Charlie let go of Bruno and faced his friend. His smile dropped into a frown. 'I had to make you stay. I couldn't lose you as well'.

Tim smiled warmly and opened his arms invitingly. Charlie embraced his friend eagerly.

Bruno and Summer joined the celebrations for a while before retreating to a more quiet area to rest.

Elzbieta had been placed in a ward and was monitored carefully while the agonising pain set in. She writhed violently as her body slowly returned to normal. Her screams were drowned out by the celebrations in the main hall.

Chapter 31

REMEMBRANCE

The suns shined vibrantly as a new day dawned in Nimara. Elzbieta walked across the hall amongst the remains of last night's party. Leftover food covered the banqueting table, and though demolished still looked impressive. She was amused to see worn-out paper hats draping chairs and hanging limply from the chandelier high above. The whole place was silent and motionless, as though time had also decided to rest. There was a sense of serenity, which soothed her, and she revelled in it. This was her moment to reflect on everything that had happened; she needed to think.

Her body had successfully returned to normal, which was a great relief, but her thoughts and emotions were still in disarray. Sighing deeply, she moved towards the window and watched the waking world. It was so beautiful out there. There was so much colour and life, and every moment she spotted something different. She could stand there for eternity and never grow bored of the sights.

Birds flitted from tree to tree, building nests or chasing each other around. Rabbits hopped in the grass, some playing and others huddling close to their young ones. A waterfall could be heard in the distance, and the river leading off from it was home to various ducks and swans who all shared the water without any complaints. The ducks paddled mischievously, loudly quacking remarks to one another. The noble swans majestically glided above the water with their heads held high as if deep in thought.

A constant theme ran through everything she had observed: togetherness. All the various creatures were in harmony with one another, and that was the true beauty of this world.

'That was very impressive of you'. Harry's gentle voice was behind her.

Disturbed from her thoughts, she jumped slightly and turned to face him. 'I did what was necessary, that's all', she replied humbly.

Harry nodded slowly and smiled. 'Even so, you were the one to save us all. We shall always remember that'.

Elzbieta felt uncomfortable with the praise and changed the topic. 'When will we go home?' Just saying the word 'home' caused her to feel desperately sad, and the thought of holding her mother tightly once more caused her eyes to moisten. Her lips trembled as she fought bitterly not to cry. She visualised a picture of her mother at home, baking in the kitchen. Although mixing dough in a bowl with all of her might, she still managed to look elegant. She smiled at Elzbieta, wiped her hands, and opened her arms for her. Those open arms were always so welcoming, and Elzbieta could not restrain the urge to run into them and let them fold around her. The delicate perfume she wore was a comforting familiarity as Elzbieta stretched her arms around her mother. Her smile turned into laughter, as she could never be as content as when she was holding her mother close.

'The ship is being prepared as we speak. Come with me; there are some friends who want to see you'.

Elzbieta allowed herself to be led into an adjoining room where Bruno, Summer, Charlie, and Tim were waiting for her. They all ran to her as she entered the room, and their joy was obvious.

'It's so good to see you again'. Summer was first to greet her and took hold of Elzbieta's hands and gripped them tightly.

Elzbieta looked from one person to another and smiled back. However, her smile was uneasy, and she found it difficult to select the right words to say.

Bruno moved closer and placed an arm gently around her shoulder. He gazed into her eyes, and his admiration for her was evident. 'We have something to show you', he told her with a voice so calm and soothing that her general posture relaxed and the frown that had formed on her face melted away and turned into a quizzical expression.

Together they all left the room, and Elzbieta was led into the garden just outside the window she had been staring out of earlier. They stopped by a gigantic tree that stood proudly amongst a sea of roses. In full bloom, the roses danced with the rhythm of the wind, hypnotically swaying from left to right, as graceful as the motion of sea waves out in the ocean. The unusual turquoise colour glittered in the sunshine, and droplets of dew held spots of light suspended on the petals. The tree itself was truly magnificent. The bark was golden and although thick, still managed to appear delicate. The leaves were shades of various greens and they too formed their own dance as they shivered when touched by the fingers of the breeze. Blossoms clutched on the branches. Their arrangement was so perfect that it would be feasible to believe that God himself had taken the time to place each flower in the right place. Stirred by the motion of the leaves, individual petals propelled towards the ground like confetti, adding to the magical scene.

Elzbieta stared open mouthed and full of awe. It was beautiful.

Charlie tapped her arm in order to capture her attention. She looked at him and smiled. Her smile was radiant and lit her eyes. Without saying anything, he took hold of her hand and pulled her towards the tree. The ground was cool and soft under her feet as they carefully stepped through the roses. Reaching the tree, Elzbieta noticed a crucifix had been placed there. It leant against the base of the trunk and was surrounded by candles. The candles were lit and amazingly fought against the breeze so that the flames stayed alive. In front of the candles was a stone tablet. Etched into the surface were the words, 'In memory of those who died that we may live'. Underneath this was inscribed, 'For Carlos, a brave soldier, a good friend, and a loving human being'.

Elzbieta's breath hitched, and she put her hands over her mouth. Her eyes became wide, and she glanced quickly at the others, who bowed their heads in a sign of respect. Tears welled into pools that gave way to streams sliding down her flushed cheeks. 'You all did this?' she hitched between sobs.

Silently they nodded.

There was a brief pause, and Bruno remarked, 'It's less than what he deserved, but he will always be in our hearts'.

'So many lives have been lost', Elzbieta added. It was evident that her grief extended to the many that had died in the battle.

'On both sides', Charlie whispered, causing the others to turn towards him in disbelief.

'How can you feel any pity for the Gwarks? They caused all this!' Summer scolded him.

Charlie raised his eyes and settled them on Summer. His gaze was direct, open, and full of pain. 'They have wives and children. They have mothers and fathers. They have loved ones who grieve as much as we do'. Lowering his head he continued, 'I have lost so much, but I am pleased that my family have gone to a better place. They are at peace. I have to carry on and somehow learn to live with the sorrow of their absence until I too die and am reunited with them. The waiting prolongs my agony. It is the same for everyone left behind'.

There was no response to this, so they all gave their attention to the crucifix under the tree and prayed for everyone that had died and for those that loved them.

Chapter 32

HOME

Harry watched the reunion from the window and began to wonder whether there truly was hope for the human race. Before meeting the inhabitants of Earth, it was believed the whole race was void of empathy or respect. Each day of their lives was soiled by jealousy, greed, and an insatiable appetite for causing pain and grief. The amount of wasteful self-destruction and, in fact, the neglect of the planet was bewildering. Their future, and the future of their generations were futile. However, these individuals had captured his heart. Their courage, acceptance, determination, and above all, love for each other ignited a spark of belief in their kind. Perhaps the few could keep their world from complete extinction.

He saw that together they made their way back to the room that they came from. Swiftly he moved away from the window and went to join them.

As he entered, Bruno, Summer, and Elzbieta turned expectantly toward Harry.

'Yes, it's time for you to return home'. Harry smiled regretfully. 'Just remember, you have created a place in all our hearts, and you will be missed'.

Bruno stepped forward and took hold of Harry's hand. At first he was going to shake it, but after a brief hesitation, he held it firmly between his own hands. 'Perhaps one day we will meet again'.

'In better circumstances I hope'. Harry nodded and placed his other hand on Bruno's, serving as a symbol of equal respect and sealed friendship. 'Bruno there is one more thing'. Harry withdrew his hands and fished out a box from deep within his pocket. 'Granddad asked that I give you this when everything was over. He believed in you and told me you gave him a renewed sense of life and love. He will always be with you in your heart and in your thoughts. Let all the knowledge he shared with you be your guide in life'.

Bruno opened the box, and inside was a golden St. Christopher medal. Bruno gave a rueful smile as he gently touched the chain that it was attached to. 'The saint of travellers', he simpered.

'Granddad will be with you every step of your journey in life', Harry added.

'What future do we have if we do not learn from those before us? Experience is precious', Bruno remarked and firmly believed.

'Stand on the shoulders of giants', Harry reminisced on the conversation he had once with his dear friend.

Bruno returned to where Summer and Elzbieta stood and placed his arm around Summer. Summer placed her head on his shoulder, revelling in his warmth.

'Are we ready?' Harry attempted to lighten the mood that had descended on them all.

They were led back to the spaceship that appeared even more magnificent, considering the backdrop of this wonderful land.

Before boarding, they all said their last good-byes. They ascended the stairs deep in thought but full of excitement to be going home.

Bruno stepped through the threshold and turned to his alien friends once more before the door closed. Charlie waved frantically, and tears cascaded down his eyes. Tim, concerned about his friend, placed his hand on his shoulder but also waved energetically. Harry, as dignified as ever, clasped his hands in front of himself and nodded.

The door slid shut, interrupting rudely and creating the final barrier between the two worlds.

'What happens now?' Summer asked, the question breaking the thick silence that held each of them spellbound.

'We go home'. Bruno was matter of fact as he put the St. Christopher around his neck.

'I don't live near you', Elzbieta realised. 'What if we are dropped of in different places?' She fumbled around her pockets and reached into the cupboard above her seat. Finding some paper and a pen, she frantically scribbled on it.

The alarm sounded for take-off. She grabbed Bruno's hand and stuffed the paper into his palm and said, 'Here, quickly, take it'.

Without asking, Bruno placed the paper in his pocket and then buckled himself in. Before another word could be said, the familiar feeling of being engulfed in the seat was replaced with nothing. They had all drifted to sleep.

CHAPTER 33

THE BUS

A JOLT THAT caused his teeth to snap woke Bruno abruptly. The familiar smell of diesel invaded his nostrils. Breathing in the dirty air again caused him to cough. Shouts and screams bellowed loudly in his ears as fellow pupils cursed each other. Some leaned over the seats to swat the person behind with whatever they had in their hands – paper, a ruler, school bags – or they threw sweets that gave off an underlying sickly sweet aroma. For a few moments Bruno felt nauseated and was not used to the hustle and bustle of everyday school bus journeys.

The bus driver muttered profanities under his breath and occasionally growled at the car drivers who dared to be on the same road as him.

Next to him, Summer took in her surroundings too. She noticed an old lady trip up on the curb, her shopping bursting out of the split bag, rolling for freedom in every direction. No one ran to help her but continued to walk on as though she did not exist.

'We're home', she exclaimed. She noticed she was back in school uniform and her school bag was under her feet. She looked at her watch and saw that it was 3:40. They were on their way home from a day of school.

Bruno surveyed the streets and noticed that in roughly ten minutes, Summer would reach her stop. He turned towards her and held her closely. Ignoring the immature whoops and cheers from those around him, he kissed her on the lips. Summer responded gladly. They released their hold on each other. Bruno grinned and looked into her eyes, gazing in admiration of her beauty. They had been through so much together and this, he found, strengthened their bond.

Touching her cheek and placing a gentle kiss once more on her lips, he whispered, 'I'm so looking forward to seeing our love grow'.

Summer frowned but did not say a word. The frown turned into a smile and she leaned forward and embraced Bruno tightly. Slowly they released each other again.

'Oh, Elzbieta!' Summer panicked.

Bruno reached inside his pocket, even though he was now in his school trousers and not the ones he wore before leaving Nimara. To his relief he pulled out the scrunched-up note. He opened it, and together they read the quickly scribbled writing.

Elzbieta Wyzcska

ElzbWyz@btinternet.com

Please contact soon, my friends.

Your friend forever. XX

They looked at each other and smiled.

'What do we do when we get home?' Summer asked, aware that her stop was fast approaching.

'Act normally', Bruno replied. 'Harry said their memories were erased so as not to grieve our disappearance. To them it will be yet another normal day of our return home from school'.

'Oh, I can't wait to see them', Summer exclaimed excitedly.

The bus sharply pulled into the stop, and Summer stood up.

Bruno moved aside to let her pass. 'See you tonight?' he asked and placed his arm around her waist.

Summer looked up at him. 'Of course. Ring me'.

With that, she skipped off the bus, eager to be reunited with her family.

As the bus sped off, Bruno sat and waited for his stop. Although things appeared to be getting back to normal so easily, he knew that deep inside he would never be the same. The boy that was taken away by the aliens that day had returned a completely different young man.

About the Book

BRUNO IS A typical fifteen-year-old boy who wants to be popular. He has a crush on a new girl named Summer, who mysteriously disappears from his life.

One very ordinary day while on his way to school, he does not reach his destination. Instead, Bruno is forced into extraordinary circumstances that test his mental and physical strength. He experiences what no one has ever had to face before, and has to make important decisions that at times are painful. It is not only his life that depends on this but the lives of a whole planet.

With the help of a handful of trustworthy and faithful companions, he must face his fiercest battle – and win. It is his destiny to fight.

Will he be victorious, or will fate deal him a losing hand?